"You find this amusing?"

"Amusing? How about appalling?" She slid from the stool, stalked to where he stood, lifted that I-dare-you chin and looked him in the eye. "Listen, and listen hard, because I'll say this only once. This baby is mine. It is not yours. You have nothing to say about how I conduct my pregnancy, where I live, what I do, or what happens after my child is born. Got that, Your Highness?"

"Ms Whitney—"

"Get out! Get out of my home and my life...I never want to see you again."

"I am the Crown Prince of Dubaac," Tariq said coldly. "And you carry my heir."

THE SHEIKH TYCOONS

by
Sandra Marton

*They're powerful, passionate—
and as sexy as sin!*

*Three desert princes—
how will they tame their feisty brides?*

THE SHEIKH'S DEFIANT BRIDE
August 2008

THE SHEIKH'S WAYWARD WIFE
December 2008

THE SHEIKH'S REBELLIOUS MISTRESS
March 2009

THE SHEIKH'S DEFIANT BRIDE

BY
SANDRA MARTON

MILLS & BOON®
Pure reading pleasure

First published in Great Britain 2008
Harlequin Mills & Boon Limited,
Eton House, 18-24 Paradise Road, Richmond, Surrey TW9 1SR

© Sandra Marton 2008

ISBN: 978 0 263 20305 9

Set in Times Roman 10½ on 12¾ pt
07-0608-46857

Printed and bound in Great Britain
by Antony Rowe Ltd, Chippenham, Wiltshire

THE SHEIKH'S
DEFIANT BRIDE

PROLOGUE

The Kingdom of Dubaac, early summer:

THE sun poured like a ribbon of molten gold from a pale blue sky.

Beneath its brutal rays, a small band of men sat motionless on their horses, embraced by the endless silence of the desert.

All eyes were on the rider whose stallion stood apart from the rest, and on the hooded goshawk that clung to his leather-gloved wrist with lethal talons.

At last, one of the men softly urged his own mount forward until it stood alongside the rider and his stallion.

"It is time, Tariq," the man said softly.

The man called Tariq nodded. "I know."

He *did* know. It was time; his father was right but, somehow, this final tribute to his dead brother was turning out to be as emotionally torturous as Sharif's funeral.

Who would have thought such an ancient custom would tear so at the heart? Tariq had been raised in Dubaac but he had lived away from the Nations for years. He was a modern, well-educated, urbanized man and this was just a symbolic gesture…

"Tariq?"

He nodded and lifted his arm. The hawk gave a little shudder of anticipation as it awaited the unlacing of its hood.

Instead Tariq undid the bird's jesses. The tiny bells that adorned the slender leather streamers fastened around the bird's legs tinkled as they fell to the sand. A second's hesitation, and then he unlaced the hood and tossed it aside.

For the first time since its captivity and subsequent training, the hawk was completely free.

Tariq lifted his face to the scorched sky, his profile as fiercely elegant as the hawk's.

"Sharif, my brother," he said huskily, "I send Bashashar to you. May you and she fly together forever in the vastness of the skies above our homeland."

Another hesitation. Then he swung his arm forward and the hawk spread its powerful wings, leaped from his gloved hand and flew unhesitatingly toward the blazing sun.

For a moment, no one moved or spoke. Then the sultan cleared his throat.

"It is done," he said gruffly.

Tariq nodded. He stood with his face still lifted to the sky, though the hawk had disappeared from sight.

"Yes, Father."

"Your brother is at peace."

Was he? Tariq wanted to think so but Sharif's sudden death was still too new. His plane had gone down on a routine flight; it had taken days to find what remained of Sharif after the crash and the subsequent fire…

"He was a good son," the sultan said quietly.

Tariq nodded.

"Someday, he would have led our people well. Now he is gone and we must rethink our plans for the future."

A muscle in Tariq's jaw tightened. He had known this was

coming, but not so quickly. Still, why put off what he knew had to be done?

"I understand, Father."

The sultan sighed. "There is no time to waste, my son."

Tariq looked at his father in alarm. "Are you ill?"

"Only if old age is illness," the sultan said quietly. "But Sharif's death is proof, as if we needed it, that Kismet rules our lives. You are my heir now, Tariq. I tremble at the thought, but if anything should happen to you…"

There was no need to say more.

The burden of succession had fallen to Tariq. And to ensure that succession, the unbroken line of rulers that stretched back centuries, it was now his responsibility to marry and produce a son.

If only Sharif had married and created sons…

If only Sharif had lived, Tariq thought, and felt the unaccustomed sting of tears in his pale gray eyes.

"Think of what has happened elsewhere in the Nations, when there has been a question about succession," the sultan said, misinterpreting Tariq's silence. "Would you wish that for our people?"

Tariq cleared his throat. "I don't need convincing, Father," he said gruffly. "I will do what must be done."

The sultan gave a faint smile. "That is good. Come now. We shall ride back to the palace and celebrate your brother's life."

"You go on with the others. I—I want to be alone for a while."

The sultan hesitated. Then he swung his horse around and signaled to his men. They rode off as they had come, single-file, in respectful silence.

Tariq dismounted. He patted the stallion's arched neck, then looked once more at the sky.

"A wife, Sharif," he said, quietly. "That is what I must find because of you." He smiled; his brother, if he could hear him, would understand this kind of banter. They'd shared it since they were boys. "And how will I do that, hmm?"

The sigh of the wind was his answer.

"Shall I let Father and the council choose my bride? You know who she'd be. Abra, who would talk me to death. Lilah, who will surely soon outweigh me."

The wind sighed again.

"Surely a man has the right to choose his own bride."

Beside him, the stallion snorted and pawed the sand.

"Where shall I find her, Sharif? In the Nations? In America? What do you think?"

Of course, Sharif was not there to answer but it wasn't necessary. Tariq knew what he'd have said.

The perfect wife would not be American.

There were only two kinds of American females: those who were flighty and interested in things of no consequence, and those who were headstrong and breathed the fire and brimstone of equality.

Neither would do.

Yes, he wanted a wife who would be attractive but there were other requirements. She would have a pleasant personality. She would be capable of carrying on appropriate dinner conversation in the circles in which he moved in a manner that would never be confrontational.

In other words, the perfect wife would understand her role as his consort but not as his equal.

A man who would one day ascend the throne needed such a woman. The truth was, any man would want such a woman. And the place to find her was here, among his own people.

The wind moaned and a tiny whirlwind of sand spun before him.

He had been educated in the States; he lived and worked there but from now on, his way of life would be grounded in the customs of Dubaac, where a man ruled his home and his wife.

A harsh cry rang out across the desert. Tariq shaded his eyes, looked up and saw Bashashar sailing high above him.

A sign, some would say. Not that he believed in signs. Still, the more he considered finding a bride, the more appeal he saw in confining his search to Dubaac and, if necessary, the other Nations.

The stallion nuzzled his shoulder. Tariq gathered the reins and mounted.

Problem solved. He would stay in Dubaac a week. Perhaps two, but no more than that.

After all, how difficult could finding a suitable wife possibly be?

CHAPTER ONE

New York City, two months later:

IT WAS not often that His Excellency Sheikh Tariq al Sayf, Crown Prince and Heir to the Throne of Dubaac, made an error in judgment.

Never in business. Even his enemies, who'd said he was too young for the task and had predicted failure when he'd taken over the New York offices of the Royal Bank of Dubaac four years ago, had to admit that the bank had flourished under his hand.

He rarely made mistakes in his personal life, either. Yes, an occasional former lover had wept and called him a cold-hearted bastard when he ended a relationship but it wasn't his fault.

He was always truthful, if perhaps a bit too blunt.

Forever was of no interest to him. He went out of his way to make that clear to women. Forever meant a wife, marriage, children—things that he'd known he must have in the future…

But the future had turned out to be now.

And so he'd stood under the hot desert sun of his homeland and told himself he would find a wife in a week. Two, at the most. After all, how difficult could that be?

Standing at the wall of glass in his huge corner office,

Tariq looked out over the Hudson River in lower Manhattan and scowled.

Not difficult at all, as it had turned out.

Impossible, was more like it.

"Idiot," he muttered through gritted teeth.

Two weeks at home had stretched into three and then four. His father had hosted an elegant state dinner to which he'd invited every high-ranking family in the country that had an eligible daughter.

Tariq had found fault with all of them.

Next, his father had hosted a dinner and invited high-ranking families with eligible daughters from all the Nations of their world. Tariq still flinched at the memory. All those young women, lined up to be presented to him, every one of them fully aware of why she was there...

He'd said "hello, how are you?"; he'd kissed their hands, made inane conversation, watched them titter and blush and never look him in the eye because young women of good reputation would not do such an outlandish thing.

He'd bought horses this same way, he'd thought suddenly, and once that image had lodged itself in his head, that was how he'd viewed them all. As mares, docilely awaiting the stallion's selection.

"Well?" his father had said impatiently, at the end of that second dinner. "Which one do you like?"

None.

They were too tall. Too short. Too thin. Too rounded. They talked too much. They didn't talk enough. They were introverted, extroverted... Frustrated, angry at himself for failing to do what had to be done, Tariq had returned to New York a month ago.

Maybe he'd been wrong about American women. Maybe

he'd find one here who would meet his requirements. When he thought it over, he'd realized he'd overlooked several things that might make them desirable choices.

On the whole, American women were attractive. All that sun, braces on their teeth in childhood, lots of vitamins and calcium…

Such things added up.

And they were socially adept, good at parties, conversant in the kinds of talk that kept people smiling but raised no hackles.

Perhaps best of all, they were in love with titles. The ones he'd met over the years had made it embarrassingly clear they'd do anything to snag a husband who had royal blood.

Of course, until now, the more obvious they'd made that, the quicker he'd fled…but that was before.

Now, an appropriate candidate's eagerness to marry into royalty was an advantage.

At any rate, he'd decided, it would do no harm to extend his search. Look around New York and see what he could find.

The answer was, nothing.

Tariq had accepted endless invitations for sails on the Sound, summer parties in Connecticut and charity events in the Hamptons. He'd taken an endless list of women to dinner, to the theater, to the concerts in Central Park they all seemed to adore despite the bad acoustics and the sullen heat and humidity of Manhattan.

He'd dated so many women that after a while, he'd run the risk of calling them by the wrong names, and where had it gotten him?

"Nowhere," he said aloud, his tone grim.

He wasn't any closer to finding the proper candidate for marriage than he'd been two months ago.

As they'd been when he'd confined his search to his

homeland, the women were too everything—including too eager to please. No downcast eyes here in the States but the intent was the same.

Yes, your highness. Of course, your highness. Oh, I agree completely, your highness.

Damn it, did he have a sign hanging around his neck declaring himself in the market for a wife?

Not that he didn't want an obedient wife. He did. Certainly, he did. After all, he would someday be the leader of his people. It would not serve his purposes to marry a woman who was not respectful.

Tariq narrowed his eyes.

Then why, once a prospective candidate seemed attractive enough—though none, to his surprise, was quite the precise physical specimen a wife of his ought to be—still, once a candidate's appearance was acceptable, why did he resort to what even he suspected were stupid tests?

He'd tell a joke that had no punch line. Make a foolish comment about world affairs. Then he'd wait, though not for long. Every time, the woman he was secretly vetting for matrimony would laugh merrily or nod her overcoiffed head like a bobble doll, and he'd look at his watch and say, "My, look at the time, I didn't realize it was so late…"

On top of that—not that he was a prude—most of them were far too sexual. Well, not exactly sexual. Obvious. That was the word. A man wanted a wife who enjoyed sex but he also wanted her to have a certain amount of reserve.

And, yes, he knew that was sexist and chauvinistic but—

But, by Ishtar, he'd dug himself into one hell of a deep hole.

Maybe that was why, a couple of weeks ago, over drinks and dinner with his two oldest friends, he'd ended up telling them about his quest.

Khalil and Salim had listened, their faces expressionless. Then they'd looked at each other.

"He's trying to find a wife," Salim had said solemnly.

"But he can't," Khalil had said, just as solemnly.

Salim's mouth had twitched. Khalil's, too. Then they'd snorted and burst into laughter.

"The Sahara Stud," Khalil had choked out. "Remember when that girl called him that at Harvard?"

"And he can't find a wife," Salim said, and they'd dissolved into laughter again.

Tariq had jumped to his feet. "You think this is amusing?" he'd said in fury. "You just wait until you have to get married!"

Shudders had replaced laughter.

"Not for years and years," Khalil had answered, "but when the time comes, I'll do it the old-fashioned way. I'll let my father make the arrangements. A prince's marriage has nothing to do with romance. It's all about duty."

Tariq sighed and stared vacantly out the window. True. Absolutely true. Then, what was taking him so long?

His brother was gone. His father was no longer a young man. What if something happened? To his father? To him? Anything was possible. Without an heir to the throne, Dubaac could be plunged into turmoil. And that must not happen. He could not let it happen....

A knock sounded at the door. Tariq swung around as his P.A. popped her head into the room.

"*The Five O'Clock Financial News* is on CNN, sir. You wanted to watch...?"

He gave her a blank look.

"To see if MicroTech would announce their new acquisition...?"

No wife. No functional brain, either, Tariq thought bleakly, and nodded his thanks.

"Right. Thank you, Eleanor. Have a good evening. I'll see you in the morning."

The door swung shut. Tariq sat down at his desk, picked up the remote control and pointed it at the flat screen TV on the wall. A couple of clicks and he was looking at some set director's idea of an office. Pale walls, dark floor, windows, a long table at which a middle-aged man in a dark blue suit sat facing three other middle-aged men in dark blue suits…

And a woman.

She wore a dark blue suit, too, but that was where the resemblance ended.

Tariq's eyes narrowed.

It was difficult to tell her age, thanks to bulky, tortoise-framed glasses with darkly smoked lenses. The glasses lent her a look of severity. So did the way she wore her pale gold hair, drawn back from her oval face in a low chignon.

She sat straight in her chair, hands neatly folded in her lap, legs demurely crossed.

They were excellent legs. Long. Lean. Nicely toned…

His belly knotted with hunger.

He could see himself lifting the woman from her chair. Letting her hair down. Taking off her glasses so he could see if she was merely attractive or heart-breakingly beautiful…

Damn it.

He was not given to fantasies about women, especially ones he had never met. Was this what his search for a wife had reduced him to? Lust for a woman on television? A woman whose name he didn't even know?

Tariq scowled.

This was what came of celibacy.

He had not been with a woman in two months. He'd thought it wise not to let a woman's talent in bed influence him in his choice of a wife.

It had seemed a clever idea.

It still was.

He just had to stop fantasizing like a schoolboy.

Tariq tore his eyes from the woman. The program's moderator, the Suit seated across from her, was speaking.

"…true, then, that MicroTech has acquired controlling interest in FutureBorn?"

The paunchiest of the Suits nodded.

"That's correct. We believe FutureBorn represents the future. No pun intended," he added with a thin smile. The two men seated with him laughed in hearty appreciation; the woman showed no reaction at all. "You see, Jay, as men and women delay childbirth, FutureBorn's new techniques will become even more important."

"But FutureBorn is in an already crowded field, isn't it?"

Another thin smile. "So it would seem. Artificial insemination has been around for a long time, but FutureBorn's new techniques… Perhaps our vice president for Marketing can explain it best."

All heads turned toward the woman. Vice president for Marketing, Tariq thought, raising one dark eyebrow. An impressive title. Had she earned it? Or had she slept her way into it? He'd been in business long enough to know those things happened.

She looked at the camera. At him, his gut said, though he knew that was ridiculous.

"I'll certainly try."

Her voice was low-pitched, almost husky. He tried to concentrate on what she was saying but he was too busy just looking at her…

"…in other words, absolutely perfect for storing sperm."

Tariq blinked. What had she just said?

"Can you explain that, please, Miss Whitney?"

Tariq sent a silent "thank you" to the moderator for asking the question. Surely the woman could not have said—

"I'll be happy to," the woman said calmly. "It's true, as you pointed out, artificial insemination is not new, but the method FutureBorn's developed to freeze sperm is not only new, it's revolutionary."

Tariq stared at the screen. What sort of talk was this from a woman?

"And the benefits are?"

"Well…" The woman ran the tip of her tongue over her lips. It had to have been an unconscious gesture but it turned his own mouth dry. "Well, one obvious benefit is that a man who has no wish to sire children at the present time can leave a specimen with us. A donation for the future, as it were, secure in the knowledge it will be available for his use years later."

A donation, Tariq thought. An interesting choice of words.

"Or, if not for his use, then for use on his behalf."

"In what way?" the moderator said.

"Well, for example, a man might wish to leave instructions as to how his sperm should be used after his death." She smiled politely. "Frozen sperm, along with proper legal documentation regarding its use, could be a twenty-first century method of ensuring a wealthy man had an heir…

Or a crown prince had a successor.

Tariq frowned.

What if he left a—a— What had she called it? A donation. What if a test tube of his semen was set aside in case the unthinkable happened and fate intervened before he'd found a suitable wife?

Hell. Was he crazy?

Tariq aimed the remote at the screen. It went blank and he shot to his feet.

A real man did not make a "donation" to a test tube. He made it in the womb of a woman.

He had not looked hard enough, that was all. In this city of millions, surely there was a perfect candidate just waiting for him to find.

He'd been invited to a party tonight. His lawyer had bought a town house on the East Side and wanted to celebrate. Tariq, imagining all the long-legged women who'd undoubtedly be there, had at first thought it an excellent opportunity. Then he'd shuddered at the realization he'd reached the point at which he thought of such things as opportunities, and he'd sent his regrets.

Another mistake, he thought as he pulled on his suit jacket and strode toward the door. First, choosing celibacy that had clearly affected his concentration. Then, refusing an invitation to a place that might, indeed, provide excellent prospects for his search for a wife.

An old American expression danced into his mind. Three strikes and you're out. It referred to baseball but it could just as readily refer to his quest. First, his search in Dubaac, then in the Nations…

Well, there wasn't going to be a third strike. He hadn't been looking hard enough, that was the problem.

And that was going to change, starting now.

"Okay, people. We're off the air."

Madison Whitney rose to her feet, unclipped the tiny black

mike from the lapel of her suit and handed it to the waiting technician.

"Madison," her boss said, "you did a fine job."

"Thank you."

"Excellent." He laughed—ho, ho, ho, Madison thought, just like an actor doing a really bad interpretation of Santa—and leaned in close. "Suppose we have a drink and discuss things?"

Discuss what? she wanted to say. *How you can figure out a way to get me into bed?* But Mrs. Whitney had not raised a stupid daughter so Madison smiled brightly, just as she'd been doing ever since MicroTech had taken over FutureBorn and said oh, that would be lovely, but she had a previous engagement.

The phony smile of her very married employer turned positively feral.

"Now, Madison, it isn't wise to say 'no' all the time."

It isn't wise to court a sexual harassment lawsuit, either, Madison thought, but she knew what he didn't, that their uneasy alliance would soon be over.

It was enough to make another smile easy to produce.

"Some other time, Mr. Shields. As I say, I have a date."

She felt his eyes on her as she walked away.

Twenty minutes later, she slid into a booth at a quiet bar on Lexington Avenue. Two things were waiting for her: a cold Cosmopolitan cocktail and her old college roommate, Barbara Dawson.

Madison sighed, lifted the drink and took a long, long sip.

"Bless you for ordering ahead. I really needed that."

"I live to serve," Barb said lightly. She smiled, and jerked her chin toward the TV screen above the bar. "I caught the show. Still hiding behind those tortoiseshells, huh?"

Madison grinned. "They make me look intellectual."

"You mean, they make you look untouchable."

"If only," Madison said, and took another sip of her drink.

"Don't tell me. The lecher's still leching?"

"Uh-huh. Did you know you were my date for tonight?"

"Why, Maddie," Barb purred, batting her lashes, "I never knew you felt that way."

"Hey, there's an idea. Maybe that'll be my next excuse." Madison shook her head. "He's impossible but then, he's a man."

"Have you ever considered it's time you stopped thinking every guy out there is a cheating, conniving jerk like your once-upon-a-time fiancé?"

"No," Madison said firmly, "because they are. And that includes my own father, who only stopped being unfaithful to my mother because he died. Men are all the same. It's a fact of life."

"Wrong."

"Right. There are no good guys, Barb. Well, except for yours, but Hank's the last one on the planet."

"Maddie…"

"Did you read the latest alumni newsletter?"

Barb looked glum. She knew where this was going. "No."

"Remember Sue Hutton? Graduated a year after us? Divorced. Sally Weinberg? Divorced. Beverly Giovanni? Divorced. Beryl Edmunds? Div—"

"Okay, okay. I get the message, but that doesn't mean—"

"Yes. It does." Madison gulped down the last of her drink and looked around for the waiter. "I am not getting married, Barb. Not ever!"

"No husband? No family? No kids?"

Madison hesitated. "No husband doesn't mean no kids. Actually—actually, I do want kids. Very much." She paused again. "But I don't want a husband to get in the way."

Barb raised an eyebrow. "And you're going to manage this how?"

Okay, Madison thought, now was the time.

"Artificial insemination," she said, and if her heart hadn't been beating so hard at this first public admission of what she was about to do, she'd have laughed at the look on Barb's face. "Surprised you, huh?"

"You could say that."

"Well, I know a lot about A.I. It's safe, it's reliable—and it means a woman needs a syringe of semen, not the man who provided it."

Something dropped to the floor. Madison looked up. The waiter, a young guy of maybe twenty, was standing next to their table. Either his jaw or his order pad had just hit the ground.

It was just what Madison needed to ease the tension.

"Another Cosmopolitan for me," she said sweetly, "another glass of Chablis for my friend...and if I dinged your ego, I apologize."

Barb groaned and put her head in her hands. "Nice," she said, once the waiter had scurried off.

Madison tried a quick smile. "Sometimes, the truth hurts."

"Speaking of which...I'm going to be blunt here, okay?"

"We're friends. Go for it."

"Well, have you thought this through? I mean, have you really considered why you want a kid? Could it be to sort of relive your own childhood? Erase your mom's mistakes? Oh, hell," she said, as Madison's smile vanished. "Maddie, I didn't mean—"

"No. It's okay. You said you were going to be blunt. So will I." Madison leaned forward. "My mother depended on the men she married for everything. I never wanted to be like that. I was intent on making my own way in life. On not having to rely on anyone, ever. Doing well in school mattered. So did getting a degree, and an M.B.A., and making it up the corporate ladder."

"Honey. You don't have to ex—"

Madison reached over the table and caught Barb's hand.

"I was sure I'd never want marriage or children, any of that stuff." She paused; her voice grew soft. "Then, one day I looked around and realized I had it all. The undergrad degree. The M.B.A. The great job. The Manhattan apartment… Except, something was missing. Something I couldn't identify."

"See? I'm right, Maddie. A guy to love and—"

"A child." Madison flashed a quick smile that didn't do a thing to rid her eyes of a sudden suspicious-looking dampness. "There's a thousand dollar Picasso print on the wall next to my desk. My P.A. has one of those school photos of her little girl next to *her* desk and you know what? It hit me one morning that her photo was a lot more important than my Picasso."

"Okay. I shouldn't have said—"

"And then, a couple of months ago, a girl who once interned for me dropped by. She had a belly the size of a beachball, her back hurt, she had to pee every five minutes—and even I could tell that she'd never been happier in her life."

Madison let go of Barbara's hand and sat back as the waiter served their fresh drinks. When he was gone, she picked up her glass.

"Right about then," she said, trying to sound lighthearted and failing, "I realized I'm going to be thirty soon. That sound you hear is my biological clock ticking."

"Thirty's nothing."

"Not true. My mother had an early menopause. For all I know, it's hereditary."

"I still say there's a man out there meant for you."

"Not if my mother's bad taste in men is also hereditary. Go

on, give me that look, but who knows? She was married three times, always to rich, gorgeous, world-class bastards. If she hadn't been in that accident, she'd probably be on husband number four."

"What about kids needing two parents?" Barb said stubbornly.

"Did you have two parents?"

"Well, no, but—"

"One loving parent is better than two who screw things up. And, yes, I know A.I. might not be the answer for everyone, but it is for me."

"You really are serious," Barb said, after a second.

"Yes." Madison gave a shaky smile. "I want a child so much…I ache, just thinking about it. The whole thing, you know? The good and the not so good. A tiny life kicking inside me. My baby in my arms. Diapers and two a.m. feedings, the first day of kindergarten, visits from the tooth fairy and in a few years, arguments about curfews…"

"Okay. I'm convinced. You actually might do this."

Madison took a breath. "I *am* going to do it," she said quietly. "I've already made the arrangements."

Barb widened her eyes. "What?"

"I've seen my OB-GYN, I've been charting my periods— and I went through the donor files at FutureBorn and picked out a guy who seems perfect."

"Meaning?"

"He's in his thirties, he has a Ph.D., he's in excellent health, he likes opera and poetry and—"

"What's he look like?"

"Average height and build, light brown hair, hazel eyes."

"I mean, what's he *look* like?"

"Oh, you don't get to see photos. It's all very anonymous.

Well, unless the donor wants his sperm kept for his own future use, of course, but when a woman purchases sperm—"

"Purchases," Barb said, with a lift of her eyebrows.

Madison shrugged. This part of the conversation was easier. Talking about the emotions driving her was tough; the technicalities were a snap.

"It's not a romance novel," she said dryly. "The purpose is to have a baby, not a relationship."

"And you're going to do this…when?"

"Monday. And if things go well—"

"Monday? So soon?"

"There's no point in waiting. Yes. Monday, two o'clock. If all goes well, nine months from now, I'll be a mother." Madison hesitated. "Will you wish me luck?"

Barb looked at her for a long moment. Then she sighed, picked up her glass and held it out.

"Of course. I wish you all the luck in the world. You know that. I just hope—"

"I'll be fine."

The friends touched glasses. They smiled at each other, the kind of smile women share when they love each other but disagree about something truly important. Then Barb cleared her throat.

"So," she said briskly, "since Monday's the big day, how about we celebrate tonight?"

"Aren't you meeting Hank?"

"Actually I thought we'd both meet Hank. His boss just bought a place on Sixtieth off Fifth, and he's throwing a big party."

Madison batted her lashes. "A party in the city in June?" she said in her very best East Coast boarding school voice. "How unfashionable."

"Come on, don't say no. It'll be fun."

"And maybe, just maybe, I'll be swept off my feet by some Prince Charming." Madison laughed at Barb's blush. "You are *so* transparent, Barbara!"

"Heck, this is only Friday. Your date with a test tube isn't until Monday."

"Very amusing."

"Come on, Maddie. If your mind's made up about this test tube thing—"

"It's not called 'this test tube thing,' it's called—"

"I know what it's called."

Madison sighed. "It's been a long day. And I'm not dressed for—"

"The party's only a couple of blocks from your place. We can stop by first so you can change. Please?"

"Sometimes, I forget what you're like when you get an idea."

Barb grinned. "Like a dog with a bone, that's me. Look, one last try at finding Prince Charming can't hurt."

"There are no princes, there are only toads."

"You're a tough woman, Madison Whitney."

"No, I'm a sucker for an old friend."

"You'll go?"

Madison nodded. She'd go, but only because it meant a lot to Barb. Come Monday, she'd put all this nonsense behind her.

The procedure would take.

She would get pregnant.

She'd have a baby, raise it alone and give it all the love in her heart.

CHAPTER TWO

By the time Tariq's taxi pulled up in front of the town house in the Sixties, he was having second thoughts.

Second thoughts? The truth was, he was on thirds and fourths.

What on earth had made him come here? He was looking for a wife, and were the chances of that happening at a summer party in Manhattan?

The cabbie looked at him. "Mister? You getting out or not?"

Not, he thought, but he was here. He might as well go inside.

The cab pulled away and Tariq looked around him. The street, bounded at either end by wide, busy, heavily trafficked thoroughfares, was tree-lined and quiet like many others in this part of the city but by the time he got to the front door, he could hear the beat of overamped music.

Finger poised above the bell, he hesitated.

It was not too late to change his mind. Strike three, he thought with a mixture of amusement and irritation, but not an important one. He'd go home, change into his running gear and head out again. A couple of miles through Central Park, perhaps he'd clear his head enough to stop thinking about obligation and duty and—

The door swung open.

One hundred and twenty decibels of guitar riff inundated

him. A brunette with a cigarette in one hand and a lighter in the other tilted her head back and flashed him a delighted smile.

"Well, well, well," she said, "such a nice package to find on the doorstep!"

She was a nice package, too, especially in a translucent dress that would have been bedroom lingerie meant only for a husband's eyes in his country but was the latest fashion in these circles.

"Isn't it lucky for both of us I decided to step outside for a cigarette right this second?"

Her smile, her voice… This was the opening gambit of a game he'd played dozens of times. A few drinks, some conversation and he'd take her home. To her bed, not his, because it was less complicated that way, whether what began tonight lasted for a few weeks or even a couple of months. And then, inevitably, he'd lose interest and she would demand to know why…

The woman moved closer. "Aren't you coming in?"

She lay her hand on his arm. He looked down at her crimson-tipped fingers, then at her face. She was beautiful but the truth was, there'd be a dozen more just like her inside. Beautiful women who'd throw themselves at him because of his looks—there was no point in being modest about what was, basically, a gift of nature that had nothing to do with him.

And when they found out who he was, that he had a title and more money than even he could comprehend…

No, he thought, he was not in the mood for that tonight.

"Sorry," he said politely, "but I seem to have come to the wrong address."

"Silly," she said, moving closer, letting her breasts brush against his arm. "You've come to exactly the right address— but if you'd prefer, we can go someplace quiet."

Suddenly everything about the situation was distasteful. Tariq's expression hardened; he shook her hand away and stepped back.

"I'm not interested," he said coldly. Her face filled with color and he told himself he was being a son of a bitch, but—

"Your highness!"

Tariq jerked his head up. One of his attorney's younger partners was hurrying toward him. Hell, he thought grimly. He was trapped.

The brunette made a quick recovery. "Your highness?" she said in a breathy voice. "You mean, you're a king?"

"It's an old joke," Tariq said sharply, "and not a very good one. Isn't that right, Edward?"

The lawyer looked puzzled. Then, to Tariq's relief, he grinned.

"A joke. Oh, yeah, absolutely." He reached out, as if to clap Tariq on the shoulder, thought better of it and, instead, made a sweeping gesture with his hand. "Come on—sir. Let me get you a drink."

"Hey," the brunette said.

Tariq ignored her and followed the lawyer into the house. It wasn't easy; the place was packed with people but, finally, they found a small patch of empty space.

"Tariq. Your highness—"

"No, please. Call me by my name. Did I get *your* name right? It is Edward, isn't it?"

"Yes, sir, it is."

"Well, Edward, this has been a very long week for me. The last thing I need tonight is to have anyone treat me with formality."

"Of course, sir." The young lawyer cleared his throat. "Mr. Strickland—John—will be delighted to see you. Let me just find him and—"

"That's not necessary. I'd just as soon wander around a bit on my own. You know, unwind."

"Ah. I get it. You want to spend the evening under the radar. Sure. Whatever you like, your highness."

Tariq thought of correcting the man again, but what for? Five minutes and he'd be out of here. Monday, he'd have his P.A. send flowers to John Strickland and his wife, along with a card thanking them for their hospitality and wishing them well in their new home.

So he smiled, exchanged a handshake with Edward and watched him melt into the crowd.

A waiter came by with a tray of hors d'oeuvres. Tariq shook his head. Another waiter, another tray. The third time, just to avoid having another tray thrust at him, he accepted something that looked like it might have flown away if a frilled red toothpick hadn't kept it anchored to a sliver of toast. He held on to it for a while, then inched toward a table and surreptitiously deposited it on a half-filled plate...

"Are you alone?"

The voice was soft and came from just behind him. Tariq turned and found himself looking at a blonde. Here we go again, he thought.

And then he stopped thinking. Logically, at any rate.

The brunette had been beautiful. This woman was—hell, she was spectacular.

Her hair was the color of spring wheat, falling in soft waves around her oval face. She had high, elegant cheekbones; her mouth was full and soft-looking. Her eyes were dark brown and bright with intelligence. She was tall and slender, her curves accented by a simple black silk dress that clung to her high breasts, narrow waist and gently rounded hips like a lover's caress.

"I said, are you alone?"

The same game, but a different gambit. Maybe he needed a break from the routine of the last weeks.

Maybe the evening was looking up after all.

He smiled, took the single step that brought him closer to her.

"What happens if I say yes?"

"If you say yes, you'll save my life."

"I'm impressed. Such high drama at a run-of-the mill party."

A quick smile tugged at the corners of her lips.

"Okay, you won't save my life but you'll save me from being unkind to a toad. Can you do that?"

"A toad?"

"A man. He just looks like a toad."

"Ah." Tariq grinned. "So, I'll get an award from the Save the Toads Society?"

The blonde laughed. Her laugh was charming, light and easy and natural.

"Something like that. Look, it'll only take a few minutes. Just talk to me. Smile. Cocktail party stuff. Please?"

"Well," Tariq said, looking serious, "if it's to conserve wildlife…"

"Wonderful. Thank you." She looked past his shoulder. "There he is," she said softly, and she flashed him a bright smile. "Oh," she said gaily, her voice just loud enough to carry beyond the two of them, "that's so true! I wouldn't have put it that way, but—" She stopped in midsentence and rolled her eyes. "He's gone."

"Toads have a way of doing that," Tariq said solemnly. "Here one second and then, hop, gone the next."

She gave another of those wonderful laughs as she looked up at him. Her eyes weren't just brown, he noticed, they were the color of rich chocolate.

"Thank you."

"You're welcome." He smiled, reached out and traced the arc of one perfect cheekbone with the tip of his finger. "What's your name?"

"My name?"

"Your name. Your address. Your phone number." His voice grew husky. "We can start there, *habiba*."

"You mean—you mean, you think…" Her face took on a hint of color. "You don't understand. I wasn't coming on to you. Seriously I'm…" She looked past him. "Oh, darling," she trilled, "yes, thanks, I'd love to!"

Tariq raised an eyebrow. "The toad is back?"

"Yes."

"If he's done something to offend you, *habiba*…"

"No. Nothing like that. I just couldn't lose him. And I didn't want to come straight out and tell him he was wasting his time."

"A woman with a heart." Tariq's voice dropped to a husky growl. "What about me, *habiba*. Am I wasting mine?"

Oh God, Madison thought, out of the frying pan and into the fire—except, this fire could absolutely burn a woman to a crisp…

And leave her thrilled it had happened.

Not a woman like her, of course. Not one who wanted no more of these silly games, but a woman who was impressed by good looks, a sense of humor, clothes that said a man had money, could definitely be in trouble any second.

And sex appeal. No point denying that. This man was sexy as hell.

Not like the toad.

He'd cornered her an hour ago, managed to separate her from Barb, or maybe Barb had done the separating. Either way, Madison had found herself trapped in a corner while he talked about himself. His success. His money. His genius in a high-tech field.

"Well, that's interesting," she'd said, when he'd paused for breath. "I'm in a high tech field, myself, and—"

She might as well not have bothered. He'd started talking again, his words silencing hers, about his expensive condo, his expensive car, his Miami pad…

"Oh, there's someone I promised to say hi to," Madison had said brightly, and she'd zoomed straight for the only man who'd seemed to be by himself.

She'd wanted a savior.

What she'd found was a man who would never save a woman from anything but would surely lead her straight into sin.

He was gorgeous. There was no other word to describe him. Tall, tall enough to still tower over her even though she was wearing spiked heels. Dark-haired, with eyes so gray they were almost silver. Broad shoulders, trim waist, long legs. He had the faintest accent that only added to his sex appeal.

He was a magnificent predator and it would be oh, so easy to celebrate this last night before her life changed forever by giving in to what was happening because she knew it was happening, that he wanted to take her home, take her to bed and she—and she—

Madison took a shaky breath and stepped back. Or tried to step back; the room was so crowded that she couldn't.

"Listen," she said quickly, "What I started to tell you a couple of minutes ago is the truth. I don't blame you for misunderstanding. I mean, it's my fault entirely, but—"

"Have we met before?"

Her eyebrows lifted. Such a trite line from a guy like this?

"No, we haven't. And as I was just saying—"

"We must have. At a party, perhaps?"

"Sorry. I just have that kind of face."

His gaze moved slowly, almost insolently over her face, lingering on her mouth with such intensity that her heart began to gallop.

"Trust me," he said softly. "You don't."

The surge of the crowd pushed them closer. Madison felt her breasts brush against his chest. Heat raced through her at the contact.

His reaction was far more blatant.

His body hardened.

She felt it, felt that swift male arousal…and felt the shock of an answering curl of desire low in her belly.

Quickly she put out her hands and pressed them against his chest.

"Thank you for your help," she said brightly.

"Planning an exit, *habiba*?"

His voice was soft, filled with sexual promise. No, she thought wildly, no, I am not going to do this, not with the rest of my life so perfectly planned.

"I am," she said in that same artificially bright tone. "He's gone."

His smile was wonderful, slow and sexy and completely male. "But he'll be back."

"I'm sure he won't."

"He will, if he has an ounce of blood in his veins. No man would be fool enough to let you walk away from him."

"Look, I don't—I mean, you don't—" Madison's gaze slid past the stranger. "Oh, hell," she said unhappily, "here he comes."

"Come on."

The man's hand—big, hard, powerful—clasped hers.

"Where?"

"Out those doors. See? There's a patio…or would you rather let the toad catch you?"

The blonde hesitated, but only for an instant.

"All right," she said, and Tariq hurried her through the crowd, through the French doors, onto the patio.

He knew damned well he could have gotten rid of her pursuer with one look but why do that when he could, instead, bring the woman here, where it was quiet and cool?

He hadn't come here looking for a night's diversion but he'd told her the truth. Only a man with no blood in his veins wouldn't want her. He was going to have her for the night. Hell, for the weekend, and nothing was going to stop him.

The French doors swung open.

The toad stepped outside.

He looked at them and his face lit.

"There you are," he said. "I've been looking everywhere. I never did finish telling you about the place I just bought in Miami—"

Tariq looked at the blonde. She bit her lip, just lightly enough to make him wish he was the one doing the biting.

"Oh, hell," she whispered.

Tariq felt his blood leap.

"Indeed," he said softly.

A heartbeat later, he had her in his arms. She looked up at him, eyes wide.

"What are you—"

"I'm making it clear who owns you tonight," Tariq said thickly, and he bent his head and kissed her.

She gasped. Her breath sighed against his lips. He made a sound deep in his throat and drew her closer.

"Kiss me back," Tariq whispered.

And she did.

Her lips parted; he slid the tip of his tongue between them, silk meeting silk, heat meeting heat, and the patio faded, the toad faded, nothing existed but the woman in his arms, the feel of her...

"Oh," she whispered, and he knew it was the same for her.

Her hands rose, flattened against his chest, slipped up and up until her fingers were deep in the thick, silky hair at his nape. She leaned into him, her breasts soft against his chest, her scent in his nostrils.

Tariq groaned.

All the taut sexual control he'd maintained for the past two months fell away. His sex hardened; he felt it leap against her and when she moaned and lifted herself to him, he gathered her closer, deepened the kiss, tasting her, letting her taste him, running his hands down her spine, cupping her bottom, lifting her, bringing her hard against him, cradling the power of his erection in the hot vee of her thighs.

Somehow, they were moving. Off the patio. Into the garden, letting the gathering night close around them, sealing them in its velvet darkness, its sweet floral scent.

The sounds of the party faded; the light spilling from the house diminished. Tariq felt something at his back. The wall of a small building. A summerhouse, screened and secluded, lit by only the softest of lights.

He drew the woman inside; she clung to him, her mouth hot and open to the penetration of his tongue, her breathing as ragged as his, her hands clasping his face as she gave herself over to the wildness of his kiss.

"I want you," he said thickly.

"Yes," she whispered, "yes..."

His mouth was at her throat; his hand was on her breast,

cupping it, shaping it, his fingertips moving over the engorged nipple that pressed through the silk of her dress and teased his palm.

"You are so beautiful," he murmured, "so beautiful…"

She slid her hand under his suit jacket, then inside his shirt. Her touch scalded him; he groaned again, grasped the hem of her dress, pushed it up her thighs.

And reached between them.

Skin. Silken and smooth. A strip of lace. Heat. The softness of damp curls…

By Ishtar, he was going to come. He, who never let passion fully sweep him away, who always maintained just enough emotional distance to observe the woman in his arms as he took her…

He was going to come.

But not like this. Damn it, not like this. He wanted to be inside her. Feel her womb close around him. Feel her legs wrap around his waist…

"No!"

Her cry shattered the stillness in the little summerhouse. Tariq raised his head, looked at her through eyes that were all but blind.

"Damn you, get away from me!"

Her fist slammed against his shoulder. It was enough to drag him back toward reality if not fully into it.

"What?" he said. "What?"

"You—you bastard! You no-good son of a—"

Madison slapped both hands against the stranger's chest, shoved hard. She could feel the panic spreading through her, not of him as much as of herself, at what she had almost done.

"Let go of me," she said. "Do you hear me? I said—"

"I heard what you said." His voice was cold. "I'm sure half of Manhattan heard what you said."

His hands fell away from her. He stepped back but it didn't

mean a damn; she could hear his ragged breathing, smell his maleness. Oh, yes, a predator, and the worst kind. Handsome. Arrogant. Wealthy. He moved in the right circles.

He was everything she despised and somehow, she'd been hovering on the brink of having sex with him. Hovering? Hell, she'd been a kiss away from it. How could that have happened?

A shudder racked her body. "You took advantage of me!"

"*I* took advantage of *you*?" he said…and he began to laugh.

She wanted to hit him again, but she was angry, not insane.

"You think this is amusing?"

"What I think," he said, "is that I probably should thank you for our little encounter. You see, I've been searching for something and now I realize it's going to take longer to find than I thought."

"I have no idea what you're talking about."

"And, also thanks to you, I just realized how easy—and how unfortunate—it would be should some woman make me give up something I must not give up, except to the right one."

"Gibberish," Madison said, folding her arms. "But I don't care. Whatever you're talking about means nothing to me."

"Exactly. And it means everything to…" He paused, frowned, cocked his head. "Of course," he said softly.

"Of course, what?"

"I just realized why you looked familiar. You're the ice princess from—what's that outfit? FutureTense?"

"FutureBorn," Madison said, "and what would you know about it?"

His cool smile faded. She could almost see his brain rev into high gear.

"Not as much as I'm going to know," he said cryptically.

"Do you know my boss? If you think you can get me fired—"

He laughed and turned away.

"You can't," Madison yelled. "I'm not going to be there long enough for that."

Tariq didn't turn around. Whatever she said meant nothing to him.

The toad was still standing on the patio. Tariq flashed a vicious smile. "The lady's all yours," he said, and made his way into the house, through the foyer, through the dining and sitting rooms, his purposeful stride attracting curious glances until, at last, he saw his attorney.

Strickland was part of a small knot of people, laughing and chatting.

Tariq stood a few feet away. "Strickland?"

The attorney looked up, saw Tariq and fell silent in mid-sentence.

"Your highness."

People turned and stared. Tariq knew the look; it was part respect, part awe, part outright envy.

Ordinarily he loathed it. Now, he welcomed it.

The blonde had made a fool of him tonight but no one else would dare.

Strickland came to his side. "Edward said you were here, your highness. I looked for you, but—"

"I need legal advice."

The lawyer blinked. "Now?"

"Right now." Tariq took his cell phone from his pocket, pressed a button and heard, as he had known he would, the voice of his personal physician answering the number that connected him to only this one patient. "Dr. Miller," he said, with the crisp conviction of a man who never has to ask but has only to command. "I am at my lawyer's home. Please meet me here in half an hour."

"Are you ill, sir?" Strickland murmured after Tariq rattled off the address and ended the call.

"Is there somewhere we can talk privately?"

"Yes, of course."

The lawyer led the way to the second floor and a handsomely furnished den far from the noise of the party.

"No," Tariq said, once the door was shut, "I'm not ill."

"Then what…"

"I wish to safeguard the rightful succession of my heir to the throne of Dubaac," Tariq said briskly, "in the unlikely event something should happen to me before I find a suitable wife. I've asked my doctor here to discuss the details but, basically, I intend to have a sample of my sperm frozen and to do it as quickly as possible. Do you foresee any legal problems?"

The attorney smiled. "None, your highness. Actually I've handled similar situations before."

"Good," Tariq said, and for the first time since his brother's death, he breathed a long sigh of relief.

CHAPTER THREE

At NINE Monday morning, Tariq left his Fifth Avenue penthouse, rode his privately keyed elevator to the lobby, declined the doorman's offer of a taxi and headed south at a brisk walk.

It was a bright summer morning but he'd have walked even if the city was gripped by a January blizzard.

He'd spent most of the night on his terrace, looking blindly into the darkness of Central Park while he told himself what he was going to do this morning was a modern version of an appointment with destiny.

A sly little voice inside him kept describing it in much more earthy terms.

Any way he looked at it, he was about to have sex with a test tube.

He was sure he'd made the right decision but it still made him wince. A healthy man in the prime of his life, a man who'd never met a woman who hadn't smiled and made it clear she was interested in more than conversation, could not possibly be in any great rush to spill his seed in the romantic confines of a doctor's office.

Saturday, he'd kept busy reading fifty pages of legalese that spelled out how his "donation" would be stored and how it could be used. He'd gone to bed with all that mumbo-jumbo dancing through his head and awakened to more of the same on Sunday.

Then he ran out of reading material.

Maybe that was why he'd had those dreams Sunday night.

About the blonde. Madison Whitney. The dreams had been intense, erotic…and infuriating. He was a grown man, damn it, not a horny teenage kid.

If he hadn't awakened just in time, he'd have found himself in a dress rehearsal for what he was scheduled to do this morning.

The only good that had come out of the Friday night disaster was that it had reminded him that he was a prince with an obligation to find a wife, not a man on the hunt for a night's pleasure.

Still, he hesitated once he reached his doctor's office.

Don't be an ass, he told himself, and he raised his chin, tightened his jaw and rang the bell.

The procedure was over in minutes.

Tariq signed some papers, stepped into a small room with a glass vial in his hand, turned down an offer of *Playmate* magazine with the arrogant assurance of a man who knows the power of his own sexuality…

And his imagination failed him. Nothing happened until he closed his eyes, remembered the woman, remembered her taste, her scent, her silky skin…

Then, only then, he'd done what he had to do.

Now, he could put the humiliation of the morning, his fury at the woman, behind him.

Madison usually began her days calmly.

Serenely, Barb had once said, with a roll of the eyes. Well, why not? Planning ahead, doing things carefully, was how

Madison had learned to overcome the uncertainties of a chaotic childhood.

Her automatic coffeemaker was programmed to turn on at six, her alarm at six-oh-five. By six-fifteen, she was always in the kitchen, showered, dressed, ready for her first jolt of caffeine. Ten minutes after that, hair blow-dried into submission, makeup on, she was ready to face the world.

Monday morning, none of that happened.

The coffee hadn't brewed. Her hair dryer died when she plugged it in. There were no clean panty hose in the drawer. Even her mascara failed her, depositing a smear of black on the lashes of one eye and nothing at all on the other.

Her fault. All of it.

The coffeepot made a carafe of boiled water, not coffee. The dryer had been at death's door last time she'd used it. Her panty hose were all in the hamper, the mascara had produced a pathetic dab of color because it was empty. Most unbelievable of all, she'd overslept because she'd forgotten—forgotten, for the first time in her life!—to set the alarm.

She'd intended to deal with all that Saturday and Sunday. Go to Zabar's for coffee, to Macy's for a new hair dryer, to Saks for mascara, wash her lingerie…

Instead she'd spent both days feverishly doing stuff that didn't need doing.

She'd cleaned cupboards and closets, floors and furniture until someone from the Department of Health could have done a white-glove inspection and come away smiling and at night, she'd watched reruns of *Sex and the City* for the hundredth time, made low-cal, low-fat, low-taste microwave popcorn and stuffed her face with it even though she wasn't hungry.

"And for what reason?" she demanded of her reflection in the bathroom mirror Monday morning.

Because she couldn't get the SOB, the stranger who'd almost seduced her, out of her head. Because even the memory of what had happened was humiliating.

Because she knew, deep down, that blaming him for everything was the worst kind of lie.

He hadn't tossed her over his shoulder and carried her away.

He hadn't lured her into that summerhouse.

He'd kissed her, was what he'd done, and her libido had done the rest, turning her into a creature she didn't know, a woman who had let a stranger do things to her that still made her blush...

That still made her bones melt, just remembering.

Damn it.

What was the sense in rehashing it all? She'd done what she'd done. It was over.

A deep breath. Another look in the mirror. A lift of the chin.

"Stop whining," Madison told herself briskly.

Who cared about Friday night? Today was Monday. *The* Monday. It was the first day of the rest of her life, the day she hoped to conceive her baby, and if that made her sound like a greeting card, so what?

It was the truth.

Madison's expression softened.

Her baby. A child to love. To nurture. That was all that mattered. Friday night, the man—not worth another second. What mattered was her appointment this afternoon and the sweet, bright promise of pregnancy. She turned her back on her reflection, went to the closet and flung the door open.

It was just that it was crazy that she, of all people, could have been swept off her feet not by a prince, as Barb had teasingly promised, but by the kind of sleazy Don Juans who'd tromped in and out of her mother's life.

He'd been good-looking but Don Juans always were. Tall.

Dark. Drop-dead gorgeous. And with an aura, a hint of some-thing in his bearing, in his speech that hinted at the exotic.

Madison snorted.

He'd probably been born in Brooklyn—and why was she wasting time on him again?

Forget the panty hose. The smooth, tamed hair. Coffee? There was a Starbucks on the corner. Concentrate on the present, not the past.

She dressed quickly. Comfortably. A white blouse. A pale pink skirt. White sling-backs with a comfortable heel, no mascara because she didn't have any, just some lip gloss, then some gel to tame her hair.

Monday might not have started well but it was going to end brilliantly. And when this was all over and her pregnancy was confirmed, she'd tell Barb Friday night's Big Lesson.

If you had to weigh the benefits of a man against a test tube, the test tube would win, every time.

No one at FutureBorn knew this was not going to be an ordinary day.

Madison, of course, was the sole exception.

How could she keep her mind on work when something so important was going to happen at two o'clock?

She watched the hands of her watch creep from nine to ten, from ten to eleven, then—was it possible?—slow from a creep to a crawl.

At noon, she opened a container of yogurt, shut her office door, took the file folder that held the data about the donor she'd selected from her locked desk drawer.

She read as she spooned up yogurt.

Yes, absolutely, she'd chosen the right man.

Educated. Healthy. Nice-looking. Polite, soft-spoken and

modest. The file didn't mention anything but education and health but she knew the rest would be true.

Excellent traits for fatherhood.

The stranger had been none of those things. He'd been a walking, talking ad for self-centered arrogance, passionate intensity and macho attitude.

In other words, he'd been sexy as hell.

Madison rolled her eyes, dumped the yogurt in the trash and put away the file.

"Are you crazy?" she muttered.

She had to be.

So what if being in his arms had been like nothing she'd ever experienced in her life?

His touch. His kisses. His hunger…and, oh, the hunger that had blazed inside her. She'd wanted him. Needed him. Another few seconds, she'd have let him take her right there, in the garden where anyone might have stumbled across them.

Let him tear aside her panties. Her thong—and what had made her wear a thong, anyway? A thong and no panty hose. A good thing, because panty hose would have gotten in his way, delayed that incredible minute when he'd put his hand between her thighs…

Madison shot to her feet.

It was barely one o'clock. Her OB-GYN's office was only a short cab ride away but there was no harm in getting there early. She was nervous and edgy. No wonder she was thinking crazy thoughts.

"Get moving, kid," she said.

And she did.

It was amazing, how something a man had dreaded could turn out to be the very thing that restored his equilibrium.

At seven that evening, Tariq stepped into the foyer of his penthouse, tossed his keys on the marquetry-topped table near the door and shrugged off his suit jacket.

He'd been so hung up in disliking what he'd had to do this morning that he'd almost forgotten the reason for doing it.

Yes, he still had to find a wife but now he could give the project the time it deserved. Choosing a woman to wed was not like choosing a date for a party. It would require planning, something he had not initially considered.

Tariq undid his tie as he climbed the stairs to his bedroom.

He would draw up a list of qualities he demanded in a wife and a list of women he already knew. Cross-reference the two. He had not considered doing that until now, either.

To solve a problem, any problem, one needed to develop a method that would lead to a solution. It was the way he conducted business; why had he not also realized it was the way to search out a suitable wife?

But not tonight.

Tariq smiled as he stripped off his clothes.

Tonight, he would take a break from his wife-search. A shower. A drink. A meal.

And a woman.

He stepped into the glass shower stall, turned his face up to the spray, turned again and let the water beat down on his neck and shoulders.

Definitely, a woman.

He'd check the names in his BlackBerry, make a call…

Madison Whitney was not in his BlackBerry.

Tariq frowned as he worked a dollop of shampoo through his hair.

Damn right, she wasn't. What man in his right mind

would want to be with a female who could turn on and off like a lightbulb?

She was a cold piece of work…except, she had been hot with passion when he'd held her in his arms and kissed her, hot with passion when he'd dreamed of her, and this morning, when he'd conjured her up, imagined taking her, entering her, hearing her cry out as he brought her to completion…

"Hell!"

Tariq turned the water to cold, shivered under the icy needles, then shut off the shower and stepped out of it.

Was he crazy, getting turned on by a memory? By a woman who had teased him almost to the point of no return?

No. He was just frustrated. A healthy male who went without sex for too long was asking for trouble—and nobody could call this morning's medical exercise "sex."

Fine. He was going to change that right—

The telephone rang as he was zipping up a pair of chinos. Let his voice mail take it… But the caller disconnected; in seconds, the phone rang again. And again…

Tariq cursed and grabbed for it.

"Hello," he barked, and this had better be—"

"Your highness!"

The attorney. Tariq sighed. "What is it, Strickland? Did you think of another fifty pages I should have signed this morning?"

"Not that, your…I…with…twenty minutes ago—knew that—and so—"

"Strickland, are you on your cell? You're breaking up."

"—yes—t-tunnel—spoke with—and nobody can explain—"

"Damn it, John, I can't hear you. Call me when you get home. Better still, wait until tomorrow and phone me at my—"

Suddenly the transmission cleared.

"Something went wrong with your donation," Strickland said, his voice as clear as if he were in the room.

Tariq sat down on the bed.

"Don't tell me I have to undergo that procedure all over again."

"No, sir. It's nothing like that. The problem wasn't with the procedure."

"What, then?"

There was a silence. Had the connection been lost again? No. He could hear Strickland breathing.

"Damn it, man, speak up!"

"Your donation was couriered to the FutureBorn laboratory, sir. Exactly as planned."

"And?"

"And—and at that point, it should have gone into storage. Instead it was—it was sent out."

Sent out? Tariq had a wild image of that damnable little vial, out for an evening on the town. Laughable, except for the sudden chill working its way down his spine.

"Sent out where?" he said, very softly.

"To an office. A doctor's office."

"Well, get it back!"

"I'm afraid that's impossible, your highness. It's been—it's been used."

"Used?"

"Yes, sir. Given to a—a recipient."

"You mean," Tariq said carefully, "you mean that some woman has been impregnated with my sperm?"

"Inseminated, sir. It would be premature to say she's been—"

"How in hell could such a thing happen?"

"I don't know, your highness."

Tariq's head was spinning. Somewhere in the vast city, a part of him had entered the womb of a stranger. If she became pregnant, if she bore a child...

"Who is she?"

"Sir. With all due respect—"

"Who is she, Strickland?"

"Your highness, there are issues of privacy here. Until I can research them—"

"Privacy?" Tariq roared, as he shot to his feet. "Some woman I've never even laid eyes on is carrying my seed and you're worried about *her* privacy? Tell me who she is or so help me, you'll regret it."

There was silence. Then Strickland cleared his throat.

"Her name," he said, "her name is Madison Whitney."

Tariq had heard that a man's vision went red with rage.

A lie.

If anything, his took on a brilliant clarity. He could see Madison Whitney as if she were standing in front of him. That coldly beautiful face, her contempt for him glittering in her eyes...

Impossible. Strickland had her name wrong. Or there was another Madison Whitney in New York.

Strickland erased those possibilities. Tariq's seed had been, as he delicately put it, "misdirected and utilized." Utilized by the very woman whose image had made Tariq's "donation" possible.

The irony was inescapable. And, all at once, so was a far darker possibility.

"She is a vice president at FutureBorn," Tariq said sharply.

"Yes."

"Perhaps she did this deliberately."

"Your highness—"

"If she knew what I intended to do—"

"Sir, it's not very likely that—"

"She would also know who I am. That I am a man of considerable wealth and—"

"And what, sir? What possible benefit could she see in it? Even if the procedure she underwent worked—and there's no guarantee it did—having your child to get at your money is a bit far-fetched—if you'll pardon me for saying so."

Tariq rubbed his forehead, where an entire assortment of percussionists seemed to have set out their drums.

"Additionally, your highness, it seems the woman had been planning this for some time. She had already selected a donor."

"A man she knows?" Tariq asked sharply, though why that should matter made no sense.

"She opted for an anonymous donor, sir."

Tariq closed his eyes while Strickland went on talking.

"I'll begin checking the grounds on which we'll sue, and—"

"Is that your best legal advice? That I should sue and let the entire world laugh?"

"The woman might choose to sue, even if you don't."

Could this nightmare get worse?

"Thus far, no one has told her of your involvement. It might not please her, any more than it pleases you."

"I am a prince," Tariq said imperiously. Later, he would recall those words and wince.

"Your highness. For now, the best option might be to do nothing."

"And if the Whitney woman becomes pregnant? Are you suggesting I let her raise a royal prince of Dubaac as a—a street urchin?"

"Hardly that," Strickland said dryly. "She's well-educated. She holds a very responsible position. She—"

"I don't care if she's Mother Teresa incarnate," Tariq

snapped. He took a deep breath, then slowly let it out. "Very well. For now, do nothing. Make sure whoever knows about this—this 'misdirection' does nothing. Is that clear?" Tariq sank down on the edge of the bed again, hand over his eyes, his clever plan lying in pieces around him "How long before we know if she is pregnant?"

"A month, sir."

"How will we get the information?"

Strickland cleared his throat. "I have ways, your highness. Be assured, we will know minutes after she does."

A month. Four weeks. Four endless weeks…

"Wait the month," Tariq said softly. "Meanwhile, have her watched."

"Sir?"

"I know something of this woman," Tariq said coldly.

"Ah. I had no idea—"

"Her sexual habits leave much to be desired. If she sleeps with another man during the next month—"

"Of course. I should have thought of—"

"But you did not," Tariq said sharply, "I did." He paused, fought for control. "Wait the month. Then, if action on our part is necessary…" Five hundred years before, the expression on his face would have been the last thing an enemy saw before his death. "Then," Tariq said, each word encased in ice, "you will visit her, and you will make it clear that she shall carry my child to term, deliver it…and hand it over to me."

CHAPTER FOUR

THIRTY days was an eternity when a man was waiting to learn if he had created life within the womb of a stranger.

Tariq buried himself in work. With meetings. With one woman after another… And found himself leaving each at her door, looking up at him in bewilderment.

He had to be up early, he said, or he had to fly to Dubaac. He had to go over some notes…

Once, he'd even found himself pleading a headache.

Pathetic.

The truth was that sex suddenly held less appeal than at any time in his life.

It was her fault, he'd think, lying awake in the small hours of the night. Madison Whitney. The ugliness of the incident in the garden, now the incredible knowledge that she carried his seed…

Her fault, that he was turned off. What man wouldn't be?

But his subconscious mind didn't seem to know it. He still had the kind of dreams a grown man should not have, and they all featured the same blonde.

And that, too, was her fault.

Thirty days went by. Then thirty-one. By the thirty-second day, he was starting to breathe easier. Perhaps nothing would come of the so-called "misdirection."

That evening, a courier delivered a letter marked Personal. Tariq took a long breath, opened the envelope…and let the air hiss from his lungs.

Madison Whitney was pregnant.

His worst fears had come true. A stranger—a woman he had every reason to despise—was pregnant with his child.

Phone me when you are ready, your highness, Strickland's accompanying note said, *and we can finalize how you wish me to break the news of your involvement to her.*

His involvement. Tariq snorted with derision. Wasn't that one hell of a word to describe his part in this disaster?

For the first time, he wondered how the Whitney woman would react to learning she carried his child. She would give it up to him; there was no question about that. He was who he was.

That made all the difference in the world.

He had a name to carry into the future. A throne to secure.

Tariq frowned.

Why had Madison Whitney wanted a child? She was a woman without a husband, a woman with a successful career and yet, she had decided to have a child. And, having made that choice, what on earth had impelled her to use artificial means?

She surely would have her choice of lovers. The investigators Strickland had hired had found no evidence of any men in her life but surely, if she'd wanted to become pregnant…

Tariq looked at Strickland's note again. *Phone me when you are ready.*

He was ready now, but not to call the lawyer. He had questions; the Whitney woman had answers and he wanted to hear them without them filtered through seven layers of explanation from a lawyer.

Tariq punched the intercom and spoke with the doorman. By the time he reached the lobby, his Porsche was waiting at the curb.

Madison Whitney's address was part of the lab report.

It turned out to belong to a high-rise building on a nondescript street on the upper East side. There was no doorman, but the lobby door was locked.

Tariq checked the nameplates on the entry wall. *M. Whitney, Apt 609.*

Now what? In the movies, he'd ring the intercom and say he was a delivery man but there was no way that would work at eight-thirty in the evening.

Hell. What was he doing here? Why put himself into a situation his attorney should handle?

He stepped back—and the lobby door opened. A middle-aged woman carrying a Maltese terrier stepped out. She smiled; the terrier yapped, and she did the polite thing and held the door for him.

Well, why not? He'd come this far. Why not see it through? So he smiled in return, said "Thank you," walked through the lobby and took the elevator to the sixth floor.

Apartment 609 was at the end of the hall. The carpet muted the sound of his steps. When he reached the door, he hesitated.

Maybe this really was a job for a lawyer.

Maybe he should stop procrastinating, he thought grimly, and pressed the doorbell.

Why did everything always happen at the same time?

Murphy's Law, Madison thought, when the doorbell rang just as she stepped from the shower.

Hadn't Torino's logged in her call? She'd ordered a pizza, then canceled it. Just the thought of all that gooey cheese had made her stomach dip. Silly, probably; it was too soon for morning sickness, even if this had been the morning…

The bell rang again.

"One second," she yelled.

Okay. So she'd eat pizza. Or throw it out. Whatever, there was no time to towel off. No time to get annoyed at Torino's for making a mistake, not on a night like this, not at the end of such a wonderful, magical day.

Riinnng!

Madison rolled her eyes, slipped on a robe, shoved her wet hair from her face and padded, barefoot, to the door.

"Okay," she said, undoing the lock, "I heard you the—"

The rest of the sentence caught in her throat.

"Good evening, Ms. Whitney."

The voice was exactly as she remembered it. Deep. Husky. And yes, definitely touched by some sort of accent. The tall, powerful body was as she remembered it, too. Lean and male and hard.

And that face. The face of a fallen angel. Cruel. Dangerous. Fascinatingly beautiful.

Madison reacted instantly, tried to shut the door but he was too quick. His hand shot out, flattened against the door and forced it open.

"Is that any way to treat a guest?"

Sardonic amusement tinged his words but his eyes glittered coldly as he looked at her. Madison's heart rose to her throat. She was naked under her robe, alone with a man with ice in his eyes. What did he want? How had he found her?

Excellent questions, but their importance paled beside the need to get rid of him.

"Stand back," she said, and congratulated herself on how calm she sounded, "or I'll scream."

"A man, an old acquaintance, stops by to say 'hello' and you scream?" He gave a soft laugh. "Not very hospitable, *habiba*."

"If you think you can frighten me—"

"Frighten you? Please, Ms. Whitney. Spare us both the dramatics."

No dramatics. He was right. Straight to the point. That was the only way to deal with him.

"What do you want?"

The amused look vanished. "To talk to you."

"We have nothing to talk about."

"Unfortunately, we do."

He brushed past her as if she were an infinitesimal annoyance. It was deliberate, she knew, a way of making it clear he would invade her space whether she liked it or not.

"I didn't invite you in!"

"No. You did not. But what I have to tell you requires privacy."

His gaze drifted over her. She knew she was blushing under that slow scrutiny. She shivered and folded her arms over her breasts.

"If you think—if you, even for a moment, think—"

"Oh, I think, *habiba*." His voice roughened. "Believe me, I think. What happened the night we met has been burned deep in my brain."

No. She would not let him draw her into talking about that night; she would not defend herself when she needed no defense.

"I don't know how you found me. Or why you've come here. But—"

"I told you, I came to talk." His gaze moved over her again. "Although, I admit, finishing what we began that night is tempting."

Her heart was pounding so loudly that she wondered if he could hear it.

"Get out."

"Believe me, *habiba*, I wish I could."

"Listen, mister—"

"Your highness."

"Excuse me?"

"I am addressed as 'your highness,' not 'mister.'"

She looked at him as if he'd lost his mind. Maybe he had. What did his title matter?

It was only that he'd expected a different reaction from her. Surprise, yes. And even fear. Well, there was that. She was white-faced and trembling; the pupils of her eyes were dilated with terror.

And yet, she was defiant.

Defiant, and beautiful.

It was clear she'd just come from the shower. The water had turned her gold hair to bronze; it tumbled wet and wild down her back. The robe she wore was old; there was nothing even remotely sexy about it—except that it outlined her damp body. The sharp little points of her nipples. The curve of her waist. The roundness of her hips and the length of her legs.

His blood leaped. He cursed himself for it. Sexual desire was not what this was about; that she should have that effect on him, even now, sharpened his anger.

"Wait a minute…"

There was something different in her voice, an awareness that matched the way she suddenly looked at him.

"You're a prince?"

Well, there it was. She was beautiful and defiant but, like every other woman he'd ever met, once she learned he was a royal, he could do no wrong.

"That's right. I am His Highness, the Crown Prince Tariq al Sayf of Dubaac."

"A prince," she repeated, except, she didn't really say the words, she snorted them on a whoop of laughter. "Ohmygod, a prince!"

"What," he said coldly, "in bloody hell is so amusing?"

"I get it now. Barb sent you."

"Who?"

"She doesn't know you and I—that we met before. And she probably thinks you're God's gift to women. Well, it's obvious *you* certainly do, and—"

He was beside her in a heartbeat, clasping her by the elbows, lifting her to her toes.

"Do not," he said through his teeth, "laugh at me!"

But she *was* laughing. She *kept* laughing, and the more she did, the more he seethed.

"Stop it," he commanded, shaking her. "Do you hear me, woman? Stop right now!"

"I can't," she gasped. "I mean, if Barb only knew the truth about you—"

"Here is the truth about me," Tariq said, and crushed her mouth beneath his.

The second he tasted her, he understood what had kept him from bedding a woman the last four weeks. It wasn't that Madison had turned him off sex.

It was exactly the opposite.

What he'd wanted, what he'd needed, was this.

This woman, in his arms, her breasts soft and full against his chest. Her belly pressed to his instantly erect flesh.

She was struggling. He didn't give a damn. He would take what he wanted. What she owed him. Take and take and take until…

Until she gave a desperate little sob, wrapped her arms around his neck, opened her mouth to his…

Exactly as she had done when she'd teased him. When she'd humiliated him.

That wasn't going to happen again.

He caught her wrists, dragged them to her sides. He slid his hands up her arms, fingers biting into her flesh as he held her from him.

A man who made a mistake once learned from it. A man who repeated the same mistake was a fool.

Her eyes flew open, wide and dark as night. She looked bewildered, but he knew better.

"Did you think you could play this game again?" he said in a dangerous voice.

"Game?"

She gasped as his grip tightened.

"Do not think you can toy with me, *habiba*, or, so help me, you will regret it."

Color swept into her face. Her mouth trembled and, for an instant, he wanted to haul her against him again, kiss her until the tremor became sweet compliancy.

A muscle knotted in his jaw.

She was good at this. He had to remember that.

"Let go of me!"

He made a show of lifting his hands from her. "With pleasure."

"If anyone's going to regret anything, it'll be you, Prince Whoever You Are, if you don't get the hell out of my apartment right now."

"Do not," he said coldly, "threaten me, madam."

"Do not," she said, just as coldly, "underestimate me, sir. You came here uninvited. I've asked you to leave. If you don't, I'm going to call the police. And believe me, that isn't a threat, it's a promise."

"You won't call the police."

She was regaining her composure. The tilt of her head, the cool smile, told him so.

"Do you think your title gives you power over me? This is America. There are laws—"

"Do you want to make speeches?" Tariq folded his arms over his chest. "Or do you want to know why I'm here?"

Madison gave an unpleasant laugh. "Trust me, your highness. I know exactly why you're here."

"You think I came for sex?" He smiled thinly. "If that were true, you'd be on your back. And I'd be deep inside you—or am I supposed to forget what happened a couple of minutes ago?"

She took a step toward him, hand raised. He caught it, enfolded it tightly in his until she gasped.

"The last time you played games," he said softly, "we were in a public place. We are alone now. Had I wanted to see the game through, I would have. Do you understand me?"

"You're hurting me!"

He glared at her for a long minute. Then he let go, tucked his hands in his pockets and stepped away. This woman brought out the worst in him. Perhaps that was her intention, to make him lose control any way she could.

He had come here for only one reason and it was time to get to it. He took a deep breath, slowly expelled it and looked at her.

"I suggest it's time you listen to what I have to say."

She answered by walking to the door and reaching for the knob.

"Goodbye, your highness."

"Madison. Damn it, I said—"

"I heard what you said. Now, *you* listen!" Her face was cold as she swung the door open. "If you ever so much as come near me again—"

"You are pregnant."

Her mouth fell open. Good, he thought grimly. He had her attention, at last.

"What did you say?"

"You found out today, when you visited your doctor."

"How—how do you know that?"

"Shut the door and I'll tell you. Unless, of course, you'd prefer to invite your neighbors to join us…?"

A second ticked by, then another. Finally she closed the door and folded her arms. Her stance was defiant but her eyes were dark with shock.

"How do you know that I'm pregnant?"

He shrugged. "Information is not difficult to acquire when you know the right people."

"Damn it, what's this all about? You're poking into my private life."

"Yes." A muscle flexed in his jaw. "Your private life—and mine."

"I don't know what you're talking about!"

"You became pregnant through artificial insemination."

"What is this?" Her eyes narrowed. "Don't tell me. You can't really think you can blackmail me into bed—"

He laughed. Her eyes narrowed; she stalked toward him and, despite everything, he found himself admiring her courage.

"I want answers, damn it! And I want them immediately." She stabbed a finger into the center of his chest. "How do you know these things about me? Why have you invaded my privacy?"

As he had moments ago, Tariq caught her hand, trapped it within his, his laughter gone.

"You have it wrong," he said coldly. "It is you who invaded *my* privacy."

"I never even knew your name until five minutes ago!"

"No," he said softly. He waited; her eyes lifted to his. "But it was my sperm that made you pregnant."

She looked at him as if he'd lost his mind. She even laughed. Whatever reaction he'd expected, it wasn't that.

"Very funny."

"Damn it, woman," Tariq growled, "this is no joke. I'm telling you the truth. There was a mix-up somewhere. I—I gave a donation of—of my semen…" Hell, this was no time to stumble over explanations. "My doctor sent it to your company for storage but it ended up at *your* doctor's office."

Her face drained of color.

"I don't believe it."

Her voice was thready. Good, he thought coldly. At least he was no longer the only one in shock.

"There couldn't have been a mistake! FutureBorn never—"

"Never be damned. It did."

"I'm telling you, it's not possible!"

"I said the same thing but it looks like we were both wrong. You were inseminated with my seed. The child you carry in your womb—"

The words wouldn't come. Thinking about it in the abstract had been difficult enough. Saying it to her was impossible.

"The child—this child inside me is—is yours?"

Her voice had gone from thready to the faintest whisper.

Tariq nodded. "Yes."

Her mouth opened, then shut. Good, he thought with harsh satisfaction. For once, he'd rendered her speechless.

"However," he said briskly, now that the worst was out of the way, "though you are hardly the woman I would have chosen to bear my son—or my daughter—the situation is easily remedied."

She was staring at him, no expression on her face at all. Good. She was taking the news well but then, she was a businesswoman. She would surely accept his settlement offer with the same equanimity with which he would make it.

How right he'd been to break the news himself. Strickland would probably still be talking his way into her apartment.

"Your child," she said. "Your child…"

She started to laugh, which he thought was odd despite her calm acceptance of what he'd just told her…except, she wasn't laughing, she was gasping for air.

"Madison?"

"I'm fine," she said.

Her eyes rolled up in her head. All Tariq had time to do was curse and catch her in his arms as she slumped toward the floor in a dead faint.

CHAPTER FIVE

IF THIS had been a movie, Madison knew she'd have come out of the faint with feminine grace, the back of her hand to her forehead, fluttering her lashes as she looked up at the dark-haired hero holding her safely in his arms.

But this wasn't a movie. It was reality, and she came to abruptly in the arms of a man she'd hoped she would never see again.

"What," she said shakily, "what happened?"

"You fainted, *habiba*."

"I never—"

"Nonetheless, you did."

His tone was sharp but she could have sworn she saw concern in his eyes. It startled her until she realized any man would be concerned if a woman dropped to the floor, unconscious.

Unconscious, because he'd told her she was pregnant with his baby.

The shock hit for a second time. The room spun; she moaned. Tariq cursed but his touch was gentle when he drew her head to his shoulder.

"Easy. Take a deep breath. Let it out slowly. That's it. And again."

Get up, she told herself. Damn it, shove him away and get on your feet...

But the room was still tilting. And—and despite everything, his arms felt like a safe haven.

His shoulder was hard, but somehow it cushioned her head better than the softest pillow.

His arms were hard, too, but they felt gentle as they held her.

Even his scent was comforting, masculine and clean.

She could hear the beat of his heart against her ear, steady and reassuring and—and—

"*Habiba*?" He cupped her face in one big hand and looked into her eyes. "Good," he said gruffly. "Some color has come back into your face."

She nodded.

"How do you feel?"

"Better."

"Are you certain?"

"Yes. Thank you, I'm—I'm—"

Thank you? Had she lost her senses? What was she thanking him for?

He had just told her the most monumental lie.

What he claimed wasn't possible. FutureBorn prided itself on running a mistake-free operation. They would never have sent her doctor the wrong sperm and this man, all ego and arrogance, would never have offered himself as a donor.

She was on FutureBorn's board. She knew the profile of what the company thought of as its typical contributors. Young medical students, struggling to pay their way through school. Scientists and artists who believed their DNA should live on into the future. A handful were simply men who understood how desperately some women wanted to conceive and contributed sperm as an act of selflessness.

Tariq al Sayf, or whatever he called himself, was not a struggling student. He was not a scientist or an artist and to think of him as an altruistic man with the good of humanity in mind was a joke.

He was the rich, self-centered prince of a country undoubtedly trapped in the dark ages.

If he was a prince at all.

New York was filled with people claiming empty titles.

So, no, she didn't believe what he'd told her. He was lying, though she couldn't imagine why he would.

And why was she still in his arms wearing nothing but a robe as thin as a handkerchief? Thin enough so she could feel his heart, beating against hers, felt his body infusing hers with its heat?

Madison jerked upright.

"Thank you for your help," she said stiffly, "but I'm fine now."

"You don't look fine," he said, and scowled. "You are pale."

"I said—"

His arms fell away from her. "I heard what you said. By all means, stand up if that's what you wish."

She shot to her feet. Foolish, because the sudden motion made the room blur but she wasn't about to give in to weakness.

She took care of herself. She had, since childhood. Right now, that meant learning why he'd told her such a monumental lie and then getting him out of her apartment and out of her life.

"What is your physician's telephone number?"

Madison looked at him. He had a cell phone in his hand. "Excuse me?"

"I want your doctor to check you over."

"That's not necessary."

He rose to his feet. He was big—six-one, six-two—much taller than she to start with but she was barefoot and he towered over her. She didn't like the feeling; it was almost as if he were trying to remind her of his power.

"You fainted," he said brusquely. "You're pregnant. You need to see a doctor."

Madison folded her arms. Ridiculous, she knew, but it made her feel taller.

"I fainted because you told me something patently impossible."

"Impossible," he said with disquieting calm, "but true."

"So you claim."

His face darkened. "Are you accusing me of lying?"

"If the shoe fits…"

"What has this to do with shoes?"

She would have laughed but she knew damned well there was nothing to laugh at.

"Never mind. It's just a saying. It means I don't know why you'd say such a thing about you and me and my baby."

"I said it because it is the truth. And because we must determine how best to handle the situation."

The situation. Her pregnancy. Her baby. And his determined insistence he was the cause of it…

"Have you had supper?"

She smiled with her teeth. "From doctors to dinner. You move right along, don't you?"

"It's a simple question. Have you eaten this evening?"

"You stormed in before I had the chance—not that it's any of your business."

"Perhaps that's why you fainted."

He took a step back, examined her slowly from head to toe with an ease that bordered on insolence. "Do you skip meals often? Is that why you're so thin?"

God, such audacity! "Listen, mister—"

"I told you, I am properly addressed as your highness." His mouth twisted. "But given our circumstances, you may call me Tariq."

"I am not thin. I am not hungry. And we *have* no circumstances, your highness."

Tariq frowned. She'd put a twist on those two words and turned his title into an insult. Normally he wouldn't blame her. Titles were archaic. He disliked them and never used his except at home, where his countrymen insisted on such outdated nonsense.

But her derision set a warning bell ringing in his head.

Americans loved titles, the women especially. How often had a woman fluttered her lashes at him and cooed "your highness" or "your majesty" and, one memorable time, "your sheikness?"

His frown deepened.

Madison Whitney was not turning out to be what he'd expected.

Beautiful women, sexy women, weren't supposed to be made of steel. They weren't supposed to look a prince in the eye and make his title sound silly or, worse, call him a liar.

Perhaps she was not going to be as easy to deal with as he'd hoped.

Of all the millions of women in this country, that this one should be pregnant by him seemed to be turning into a cosmic joke.

"I'll give you two minutes to explain yourself," she said briskly. "After that, you're history."

Her chin was lifted at an angle that could only be called pugnacious. Her face was bare of makeup. Her robe was a joke, her feet were bare, her hair had dried into wild waves…

And still, she was magnificent. Not just beautiful but brave and proud, and by Ishtar, he could feel it in his bones. She was definitely going to give him trouble.

"You've already wasted a minute."

"I told you why I'm here, *habiba*. You just refuse to accept the explanation."

"That crazy story?" She snorted. "Try again, Mr. Prince!"

His jaw knotted. Such insolence!

He wanted to grab her and shake her—or grab her and kiss her. Silence her as he had that night in the garden, as he had a little while ago by covering her mouth with his, kissing her until she sighed with passion. He'd carry her into the bedroom, fill her womb with his seed the way it should have been done...

Tariq muttered a short, succinct word, turned on his heel and strode into the kitchen.

"Hey. Hey! What do you think you're doing?"

"I'm going to make you some toast and tea. Once you've eaten, we'll talk."

"I do not want toast or tea, I do not want to talk and I certainly do not want you in my kitchen."

Speaking to the wall would have made more sense. Madison glared at the man who thought he could take charge of her life as he flung open cupboard doors.

"Where do you keep the tea?" He glared at her. "Herbal tea. Pregnant women do not use caffeine."

What did he know about pregnant women? Did he have a wife? For all she knew, he had a harem.

"Lovely," she said brightly. "I see that you're an expert on pregnant women."

"Are you asking if I am married?"

Color swept into her face. "Why would I care?"

"For the record, I have no wife. I have no children. I do

have female cousins and female friends. I am aware of these things. Now, where is the tea?"

Stiff-necked, arrogant bastard! What was the sense in arguing? She'd never get rid of him that way. The best plan was to let him play amateur chef and then throw him out on his royal tail.

"Bottom shelf, over the sink," Madison said coldly. "And I like my toast lightly buttered."

To her surprise, he laughed. "Yes, ma'am."

Grumbling, she flung herself onto a stool at the counter and watched him move around her kitchen, taking bread from the fridge, selecting a tea bag from the canister—she noticed that he didn't bother asking if she wanted orange blossom or green apple but then, why would he when he was sure he had all the answers?

God, she despised him! To think that he, of all the men on file at FutureBorn, should have fathered her baby…

Sired. Not fathered. *Sired.* There was a big difference.

Besides, he hadn't. She was positive of it. He didn't need the money, didn't have a selfless bone in his hard, gorgeous body.

Why, then, would he tell her the baby was his?

"Why?" she blurted, because, despite what she'd just told herself about waiting, she couldn't stand it another minute. "Why have you come here? Why the fantastic story? What reason could you possibly have for—"

He set a plate in front of her. Buttered toast, with a dollop of strawberry jam alongside.

"Eat."

She glared at him, saw that tight jaw, the icy eyes, and decided doing as he said might be a good idea. She really was starving, even maybe a little light-headed, and after all, she was eating for two now.

She picked up a piece of toast, slathered jam over it and bit in. The prince-turned-chef put a mug of steaming tea beside the plate.

"You have no honey," he said accusingly, "only white sugar, which is not good for you or the child."

Madison batted her lashes.

"How nice," she said sweetly. "A prince. A cook. And a medical expert. Lucky me, having you stop by."

He probably thought so, anyway. He probably thought himself a gift to womankind, and his DNA a gift to the world. Even the way he stood beside the counter, hip-shot, arms folded, face expressionless as he watched her, spoke of supreme self-assurance.

Such nonsense, his claim that he'd donated sperm—but if he had, the woman who got it would be lucky, assuming she put any store in a man's looks.

Despising the sheikh of Dubaac didn't mean she was blind.

Women probably fell at his feet. Even she, before she'd wised up to him. She'd made a fool of herself, letting him kiss her, touch her, until all that mattered was the feel of his hands, the taste of his mouth.

The only "donation" a man like him would make would be in bed, with the woman beneath him begging for his possession.

"Whatever are you thinking, *habiba*?"

Madison's gaze flew to him. His voice was low and rough; those gray eyes glittered like silver. If she hadn't known better, she'd have sworn he'd read her thoughts.

The air between them seemed to thicken. She wanted to look away but she couldn't.

"There's jam on your lip." His voice was rough.

"Where?" she said, the word barely a whisper.

"Right—there," he said, and leaned toward her.

She felt the whisper of his breath. The fleeting touch of his tongue. Her eyes closed; a murmur rose in her throat…

She jerked back. So did he. He turned away but not before her gaze swept down his body, to where the softly-faded denim of his jeans cupped the sudden tumescent bulge of his sex.

He wasn't the only one.

Heat bloomed between her thighs. She could feel the almost painful budding of her nipples against the thinness of her robe.

Had he noticed? She wanted to cross her arms over her breasts but that would only draw attention to what had happened.

How could a kiss have such an effect?

Carefully she picked up the napkin and wiped her lips. She waited until her heartbeat steadied. When she looked up again, Tariq was at the sink, rinsing dishes as if he did things like that every day of his no-doubt useless life.

"All right," she said briskly. "You've done your Good Samaritan act. You made tea and toast, cleaned up after yourself and I'm feeling much better. Thank you—and now, go away."

He shut off the water. Dried his hands on the towel hanging beside the sink and then turned and looked at her. What had happened a moment ago might never have taken place; his eyes were the cool eyes of a stranger.

"You mean, now, we talk."

"Fine." Madison folded her hands on the counter. "Talk, then. Just don't take too long to come up with a convincing explanation of why you came here tonight."

"I've already told you that."

She sighed. All at once, she was exhausted. It had been a long day, starting with the exciting news from her doctor and ending with Tariq al Sayf's intrusion into her life.

"Yes. You have. So let me tell you why what you claim is impossible—assuming you really are a FutureBorn donor."

"That is not how I would describe it."

"How *I* would describe it is that I carefully selected a donor from the files. You, your highness, are not that man."

His lips curved in a mirthless smile. "I certainly did not intend to be."

"My selection was—is—a perfect match for my requirements."

For her requirements, Tariq thought. Interesting, that she should have thought of a father for her child in the same terms as he had thought of a woman to bear him an heir.

"I chose a man who was gentle. Easygoing. An intellectual, with creative leanings."

Another quick, dangerous smile.

"And here I am, instead. A barbarian from a land you never heard of. Cruel. Unfeeling. About as intellectual as a game of rugby. That's what you're thinking, isn't it?"

Why lie? Madison shrugged. "You said it, not me. And besides all that, I don't really see you as a do—" She frowned as he took an envelope from his back pocket and tossed it on the counter. "What's that?"

"Open it."

She looked from the envelope to him. His expression gave nothing away; the very absence of emotion in his eyes had more meaning than anything he'd said until now.

"It won't bite you, *habiba*. It's a letter from my attorney. I suggest you read it before you say anything else."

She didn't want to. She didn't even want to touch it. For some crazy reason, her thoughts swung back to childhood, to an old ditty about what evil would befall you if you stepped on a crack in the sidewalk.

She'd never believed stuff like that. Her childhood had not lent itself to silly superstitions. Still, she had the awful feeling that if she picked up the envelope, read the letter inside it, she'd somehow unleash the hounds of hell.

"Read it," Tariq said, and there was no way on earth to ignore that command.

The envelope was of ivory bond, heavy and rich to the touch. The single page within it was the same.

The engraved letterhead sent her heart skittering into her throat.

Strickland, Forbes, DiGennaro and Lustig, Attorneys at Law.

She knew the name. Anyone who did business in New York would. There were bad law firms and good law firms. There were those that were excellent, and those people talked about in tones of hushed reverence.

And then there was Strickland, Forbes, DiGennaro and Lustig. The firm was almost as old as the city; its reputation had never been touched by scandal, and the blood of its clients was the bluest of blue.

They would not represent a bogus prince, and they would not support a bogus claim.

Madison's throat constricted. She stared blindly at the paper.

"Shall I read it to you?"

Her head came up. The prince was watching her the way a cobra would watch a hapless mouse.

"No," she said, and then she cleared her throat. "Surprisingly enough," she said with what she hoped was a careless smile, "I'm capable of doing that for myself."

At first, the words were a blur. Then, gradually, they came into focus.

Your most respected excellence, Prince Tariq al Sayf, Crown Prince of Dubaac, Heir to the Throne of the Golden Falcon. Greetings.

Okay. So he had a real title. What did she give a damn about titles?

...reference to our earlier conversation...

Legalspeak filled the next paragraph. Madison felt the tension easing. An abundance of legalspeak often meant an abundance of crapola.

Unfortunately I must tell you that our concerns have been confirmed. Despite our legal directives, errors of significant magnitude...

Her vision blurred again. She took a breath, waited, then continued reading.

FutureBorn admits that the semen of your highness, Prince Tariq al Sayf, which was to be kept for use only by you or those duly authorized to act on your behalf, was inadvertently delivered to Jennifer Thomas, M.D., and introduced into the womb of Ms. Madison Jane Whitney who resides at...

The letter fluttered to the counter.

Introduced, Madison thought, and felt the bite of hysterical laughter in her throat. Introduced, his sperm to her womb.

She looked up. He was watching her as he had before, with a frigid clinical interest. Without volition, her hands folded over her flat belly.

"I told you the truth, *habiba*. I am not in the habit of telling falsehoods."

The sanctimonious son of a bitch! His only concern was that she hadn't believed him. What about *her* concerns? *She* was the one who'd been deceived. He was only the donor; she was the woman who'd wanted a child...

Except, the letter had inferred something else. She picked it up, read again the paragraph about his sperm being stored for use only by him.

Madison lifted her head.

"But—but what does this mean? It says you didn't intend to have your—your—" It was foolish, but she couldn't bring herself to say the word. "You didn't intend your donation for anonymous use?"

He flashed a thin, unpleasant smile. "I make donations to the Boy Scouts. To the ASPCA and to the Nature Conservancy. Not to sperm banks."

"Then, why…"

His expression hardened. "That is my business."

"Your business?" The hysterical laugh she'd suppressed burst from her throat. "Your *business*, Prince Tariq, is inside me! I think that makes it my business, too."

Was she right?

Tariq scowled, went to the stove and began brewing a mug of tea he didn't want. Anything, to give himself time to think.

He had to admit that this was a difficult situation for her. Not as fraught with problems as for him, of course; she was not attempting to safeguard the future of a nation but still, she had wanted one kind of man to sire her child and, instead, she had him.

There were women who would kill to trade places with her but he knew she'd probably laugh in his face if he told her that.

She was fearless.

Fearless, and beautiful, and bright. So, why had she turned to a sperm bank? Surely she could have any man she wished. Why wasn't she married? At the very least, why hadn't she asked a lover for his seed?

He could surely ask her that.

"I have questions, too," he said, turning toward her.

"For instance?"

"Why aren't you married? Why did you choose to have a child by using the sperm of a stranger?"

Color swept into her face but she didn't flinch.

"I could give you the answer you just gave me, that it's none of your business, but what would be the point? I'm not married for the same reason I used a sperm bank. I don't believe in marriage or relationships." Her chin lifted. "Is that clear enough for you?"

It was not. A woman who turned to fire in a man's arms was meant for sex, not for syringes and test tubes...but he knew better than to say so. He needed her cooperation, not her animosity.

"Now it's your turn, your highness. Why did you turn to FutureBorn?"

A muscle knotted in his jaw. Perhaps she was entitled to an answer.

"For my people."

She blinked. "I don't understand."

"I am the son of the Sultan of Dubaac. My father has—my father *had* two sons. My brother, Sharif, and me." He paused; it still hurt to say the words. "Sharif died in an accident some months ago. He was not married, he had no children, left no heir, which means I am now the successor to the throne of the Golden Falcon."

"And?"

"And though I tried, I could not find a suitable wife. It must be done quickly, you see. My father is in good health but no one can predict the future and if something were to happen to him and then to me..."

Why was he telling her all this? Her question was simple; so should have been his answer.

Tariq drew himself up.

"Banking my seed seemed a wise move." His mouth thinned. "But FutureBorn made a mistake."

Madison gave a weak laugh. "The understatement of the century."

"And I have come here tonight to remedy it."

She looked at him with interest. "How are you going to do that?" Her expression turned icy. "If you think I'd do anything to stop this pregnancy…"

"I would never ask such a thing!"

"Good, because—"

She paused. He was dragging yet another envelope from his pocket. "Another letter?" she said warily.

Tariq smiled. "The resolution to our problem." He took a sheet of paper from the envelope and laid it on the counter. "I will, of course, pay for your medical care."

"What? No. I don't need that. I don't *want* it! This baby is—"

"And your living expenses. You will not work during your pregnancy. That is a given."

She stared at him. "I don't think you get it, Prince! You have nothing to do with—"

"Once my heir is born, you will take proper care of him." He looked around, as if seeing her place for the first time. "Your quarters are acceptable but I would prefer moving you to a larger apartment—"

"Are you crazy?"

"One with room for a nanny, though I expect you to provide primary care for the child."

Madison laughed. He felt his face heat with rage.

"You find this amusing?" he said, his tone silken.

"Amusing? How about appalling? How about, are you as dense as you seem?" She slid from the stool, stalked to where he stood, lifted that I-dare-you chin and looked him in the eye. "Listen and listen hard, because I'll only say this once. This baby is mine. It is not yours. You have nothing to say about how I conduct my pregnancy, where I live, what I do, or what happens after my child is born. Got that, your highness?"

"Ms. Whitney—"

"Get out! Get out of my home and my life. You are a horrible, impossible man and I never want to see you again."

"I am the Crown Prince of Dubaac," Tariq said coldly. "And you carry my heir."

"The hell I do!"

"Ten million dollars." She stared at him, her expression blank. "Very well," he said grimly. "Twenty million."

"For what?"

"That is what I will pay you on my child's first birthday, when he is old enough to leave his mother. You will, of course, have visitation rights—"

He saw the blur of her fist as she swung but there was no time to sidestep. She caught him square in the eye and, to his amazement, rocked him back on his heels.

"You—you evil, miserable, self-important son of a bitch!"

She flew at him again; he grabbed her by the wrists, which wasn't easy because his eye hurt like hell. Damn it, how could this slip of a female have managed a punch like that?

She was panting, struggling to get free. He was half-blind so he did what boxers do when they're on the ropes—threw his arms around her, used his body to immobilize her and keep her from doing more damage.

"This is my baby, you pathetic bastard! Not your heir. Not a—a thing to be sold! And if you try to take my child, the least I'll do is see to it that you rot in jail for the rest of your life."

"You're an intelligent woman," he said, giving it one last try. "Stop and think. You're young, obviously fertile. You can always have another child."

"How about you having another brain? I want *this* child. I love my baby. You hear me, your lowliness? I-love-my-baby!"

Tariq frowned.

Of all the things he'd considered, he'd overlooked that possibility. He wanted a child because of his commitment to his people. She wanted one because she had those female hormonal instincts.

It had not dawned on him to factor love into the equation.

His mother had been a perfumed figure who'd drifted in and out of his life and Sharif's. She'd seemed pleased with them, but love…?

"Love?" he said.

"Love," Madison said fiercely.

Tariq's frown deepened.

If this were his country, he would simply command her to do as he wished—but this was America, she was American and she had a sentimental view of things.

Strickland had already warned him there was no case law to fall back on, no situation he could find in which a sperm donor and the recipient of that sperm both wanted custody of the resultant offspring.

Now what?

A long, drawn-out, scandalous legal battle? The whole embarrassing story splashed across the gossip columns? The media vultures would feed on the story for months.

His reputation would be ruined. Far worse, his father, his people, his country, would be humiliated. And no matter how the case ended, the child, his heir, would forever be the butt of a thousand terrible jokes.

The woman was still fighting him, twisting and struggling in his arms. It was impossible not to be aware of her. The softness of her breasts. The thrust of her hips. Even the smell of her, sexy and female…

Despite everything else—his anger, her intransigence, the legal quagmire he'd stepped into—his body was responding.

He was growing hard. *Growing* hard? He was already so erect he was like stone.

And she knew it.

Suddenly she became absolutely still. Her face lifted to his; he tried to read the dark mix of rage and fear in her eyes but it was impossible.

He only knew there was something else there, too.

Hunger.

He groaned. Brought her hand to him. Let her feel what she had done to him. And when she gave a hot little cry, he brought his mouth to hers. Kissed her, kissed her without mercy. She hissed like a wildcat. Her sharp teeth sank into his bottom lip. The taste of blood, of anger, of something darker and even more primitive was in his mouth and then her tongue was dancing against his, her hands were in his hair, she was kissing him back and moving, moving against him.

He slid his hands inside her robe.

Cupped one breast. Caught his breath as the nipple budded under the brush of his thumb. As she cried out and lifted herself against him.

"Yes," he said thickly, "yes…"

His hand moved down her body, over her belly, brushed over her mons. She cried out again and as he kissed her, she sucked the tip of his tongue into her mouth.

Tariq grabbed the lapels of her robe. Jerked them open. Began pushing the robe from her shoulders but suddenly, she went crazy, pulled away from him, slammed her fists against his chest.

"No," she said, her voice trembling, "no, no, no!"

He didn't listen. Couldn't listen. He wanted this, had to have this… And then she said "no" again and this time he was the one who jerked back, his breathing ragged.

She had played this game with him before.

"Get out!" she whispered. Her voice trembled. "Do you hear me? Get out!"

He stared at her and thought how easy it would be to finish this. He could carry her to the bed, show her what happened when a woman teased a man beyond endurance.

But the stakes were too high.

There was a new playing piece on the game board: the child they'd created together without sex, without emotion. The child she would not give him and he could not permit her to keep.

He turned away, ran his hands through his hair, forced himself to calm down. Then he swung toward her, his face a mask.

"I will not take the child from you," he said, his voice rough and harsh and suddenly shot with the accent he had surely lost, years ago.

"No," she said with conviction, "you most assuredly will not!"

"What I *will* do," Tariq said, with the assurance of a man who'd just solved the riddle of the ages, "is take you as my wife."

CHAPTER SIX

RUGGED cliffs rose above the Hudson River.

In the small hours of the night, the road that traversed those cliffs was almost deserted. Though the place was little more than an hour from the heart of Manhattan, Tariq could almost imagine he was racing his Porsche on a cliff above one of the wide mountain rivers of Dubaac.

His foot was almost to the floor; last time he'd bothered checking, the speedometer needle hovered at one-forty. It was a dangerous speed for a dangerous road, which made it perfect for a man still filled with a savage rage.

He had proposed marriage and Madison Whitney had laughed in his face.

His hands tightened on the wheel.

At first, he'd thought the expression on her face was one of shock. Who would have blamed her? He'd shocked himself but then, what other choice was there but marriage?

Whatever he'd expected, it wasn't laughter.

"Me?" she'd said. "Marry you?"

Who did she think she was? She wasn't expected to spin straw into gold, for Ishtar's sake! He wasn't Rumpelstiltskin. He was a sheikh. A prince. And he'd offered to make her his wife!

Fury had surged through him. He'd grabbed her by the elbows, hoisted her to her toes, imagined shaking her until her teeth rattled…

Imagined something far more primitive. Carrying her to the bed. Tearing off her robe. Taking her again and again until her laughter turned to cries of passion, until she understood the consequences of taunting a man until she'd stripped him of the last vestiges of self-control.

But he hadn't.

He'd hung onto just enough sanity to wonder if that wasn't exactly what she wanted, that she'd revel in turning him into a beast instead of a man.

He'd spat out a name for women like her, shoved her aside and stormed from her apartment.

Now he was on this road, letting out his anger and frustration, the Porsche as responsive to his touch as the woman had been…

And who in hell gave a damn about that?

He would never deliberately choose a wife like Madison Whitney. So what if she was beautiful? The world was filled with beautiful women. So what if she had him dancing on a sexual tightrope? He knew scores of women who would happily sate his hunger.

Why would he want a wife who played sexual games? Who teased and taunted? Who went from sex-kitten to defiant wild-cat in a heartbeat?

The road made a sharp turn. He took it without slowing down, finding satisfaction in the squeal of the tires and rush of adrenaline that came with the knowledge that he had sufficient control over the Porsche to keep it from skidding over the edge of the cliff.

If only he could control this damnable female the same way.

Still, he'd been willing to deal with that. She was not his idea of a wife but what choice did he have?

He wanted his child.

And he could change the woman.

He had trained horses and dogs and birds of prey. Not that training a woman would be the same: he was a modern man, fully aware of women's rights but, after all, the same principles would apply.

There'd be rules. Goals. Rewards for good behavior and penalties for anything that wasn't.

She'd balk, but she was intelligent. She'd learn quickly enough and then everyone would benefit. His people would have their heir, his child would have its birthright and Madison would have a husband.

That was obviously what she needed. A husband to tame her. That she'd even thought to have a child without a husband spoke volumes about the kind of obstinate, stubborn woman she was.

He eased his foot off the gas pedal, let the car's speed drop until the dark trees no longer flashed by and swung into what a sign identified as a scenic overlook. Then he let down the windows, shut off the engine and let the night breeze cool his flushed face.

Madison carried his child. *His* child, and he would not be locked out of its life.

The question, he thought, tapping his fingers against the steering wheel, the question was, what could he do about it?

There was no point in calling Strickland for legal advice. The man had already made it clear he didn't have any. Besides, he had no intention of telling him that he'd asked Madison to marry him and she had laughed in his face.

He'd be damned if he'd tell that to anyone.

Tariq heaved a sigh.

He was a man of this century in all possible ways. He traveled by private jet; his life was organized around his BlackBerry. He could not imagine life without computers and cell phones.

Still, there were times he could see the benefits in the old ways.

Centuries ago, if a man of his people wanted a woman who didn't want him, all he had to do was kidnap her, sleep with her, then state, publicly, that he had made her his wife.

Vestiges of the custom lived on, even today.

A groom might carry off his bride on their wedding night. It was done in fun, to the cheers of the guests and with the bride pretending to fight her kidnapper.

Actually, among some of his people, those who clung to the old ways, it was still all that was necessary for a marriage to be legal…

Tariq's fingers stilled on the steering wheel.

No. It was crazy. It was insane…

It was the only option he had.

He turned the key. Peeled out of the parking area. Raced back to the city, to his penthouse and began making phone calls, never mind that it was after one in the morning. A prince had privileges. He never took advantage of them, no matter what Madison inferred, but he did, now.

An hour later, it was done.

His pilot, his P.A., the florist he'd used so many times before… Yes, they all said, what he asked was not a problem, with the florist adding that she'd never heard of anything more romantic.

Romantic, indeed, Tariq thought coldly as he ended the last call.

Let the Whitney woman laugh now, he thought, and when he tumbled into bed, he slept the sleep of a man who knows he's done the right thing.

Forced to do it, perhaps…but the right thing, nonetheless.

Madison slept hardly at all.

She tossed and turned and thought about the arrogant, insolent, vile, let-the-peasants-eat-cake prince.

He'd really imagined his title would impress her. That she'd curtsy and bat her lashes and say, *Oh, yes, your majesty, of course I'll sell you my baby*. And when that hadn't happened—shock, shock, shock—he'd said, well, if she wouldn't do that, then he'd take her as his wife.

Take her, as if she were for sale!

"Think again," she muttered to the darkened bedroom.

Okay. So he was upset. So he hadn't expected his sperm to be given away. So what? She was upset, too. You made plans, you chose The Perfect Donor and what did you end up with?

The Prince from Hell.

Sure, he was upset, learning what had happened, that she was carrying his child—but it *wasn't* his child. She was the one who'd arranged for the insemination, the one with a tiny life in her womb, the one whose body would nurture that life for the next eight months.

His part was over with. Besides, he had no legal rights. That was part of the FutureBorn agreement. The donor remained unknown…

Except, that wasn't what had happened. The prince had not actually been a donor; he'd set his sperm aside for future purpose—and why would a man so incredibly beautiful, because that was the only way to describe all that dark hair, the pale gray eyes, the hawklike intensity, the hard body—

why would a man who looked like that need to store his seed in a test tube when surely any woman he wanted would...

Damn it!

Madison sat up. Switched on the bedside lamp. Folded her arms and glared at the wall.

She would never give him her baby.

She would never marry him.

But if he behaved like a human being instead of a tyrant, if he agreed to certain terms, she might permit him some contact with the child his sperm had sired. Four visits a year. Six, if he conducted himself well. Dealt only with the child and didn't do more than say hello to her.

Didn't kiss her.

Didn't put his hands on her. On her breasts. Between her thighs...

Madison trembled, shut off the light and sank back against the pillows. Maybe she'd give him visitation rights. Maybe she wouldn't. When morning came, she'd decide.

The day started well.

Her alarm went off on time; the coffeemaker did its thing and so did her new hair dryer.

While she dressed, she debated what to do about the prince. By the time she reached her office she still hadn't decided. Then she stepped from the elevator and found most of her people waiting for her, their faces radiant with delight.

So exciting, they said. *Awesome*, they said. *Tell us the details, they said*.

Madison blinked. Did the entire world know she was pregnant?

But it wasn't that.

It was the flowers.

THE FLOWERS, she thought in amazement, caps all the way. Vases of them. Roses in a dozen colors. Tulips in a dozen more. Baskets of violets. Of mums. Of tiny, gorgeous orchids. There were flowers everywhere, filling her office, overflowing into her P.A.'s cubicle.

And a hand-written note in a sealed envelope.

Dear Madison:

I hope you can find it in your heart to forgive me for my behavior last night. I was rude and insensitive, and the only excuse I can offer is the shock I felt on discovering the error that so deeply affects us both.

I would be grateful if you would agree to have lunch with me today. We can discuss our situation calmly. Be assured that I fully understand that you have no wish to accede to my impetuously made requests, and that I look forward to finding a more sensible solution that will benefit you, me and, most importantly, the child.

I will send my car for you at noon. And, again, please forgive me.

Sincerely yours,

Tariq

She looked up. Everyone was grinning. They thought all this was from a new boyfriend.

Let them think it.

As for the prince's apology…she'd accept it. Hadn't she already tried seeing the news of her pregnancy from his point of view?

He was thinking rationally. They'd have lunch and talk, she'd grant him some visitation rights, and that would be that. She'd have to figure out how to tell her child, when it was old enough, that his—or her—father was a prince, but that wouldn't be any more difficult than explaining how it had been conceived in the first place.

It might even be easier.

Anything was possible.

Promptly at one, Madison slipped into the glove-leather comfort of an enormous black Bentley sedan. The chauffeur closed the door, then got behind the wheel.

"For madame," he said, and handed her an envelope.

The car glided into traffic as she took the note from the envelope and read it.

It was brief and apologetic. Tariq regretted it, but a sudden business problem meant he had to fly to Boston. He hoped she would be willing to keep their lunch appointment anyway, since he would be out of town for the next several weeks and he wanted to get this settled.

His driver was taking her to the airport; they would eat on his plane. She could spend the afternoon in Boston or his pilot would fly her home immediately.

I apologize for the change in plans.

Madison frowned. So many apologies from a man she would have sworn had never offered one in his life...

A tingle of apprehension danced across her skin but, really, what was there to be apprehensive about? In the prince's world, lunches on his plane were undoubtedly commonplace.

Why not go along with what was, after all, an efficient arrangement?

His plane was waiting on the tarmac, in a section of Kennedy Airport that was new to her.

The fuselage bore the image of a fierce golden hawk with the words *Kingdom of Dubaac* engraved below its talons. It was, Madison realized, a royal crest.

Somehow, that changed things—and wasn't that ridiculous? A private plane was exactly that. What did it matter if it was a corporate jet or a royal one? Still, she hesitated as the driver opened the limousine's rear door.

"Madame?"

She looked at the outstretched hand. The unrevealing expression. *Don't*, a tiny voice inside her whispered but she ignored it, accepted the driver's hand and walked to the plane.

An attendant waited at the foot of the steps.

"Ms. Whitney," he said pleasantly. "How are you today?"

A second attendant smiled as Madison stepped through the door to the cabin.

"Welcome, Ms. Whitney."

So many welcomes. So many polite smiles. So much grandeur, Madison thought, and caught her breath.

She had flown first-class many times on business but this—this was another world. Deep blue carpeting stretched the length of the cabin; cream-colored leather love seats and chairs were arranged in small groupings. A smoked glass table, set for two, stood between two of the chairs. Flowers. White linen napkins and place mats. Gleaming china and flatware…

"Madison."

And coming toward her was Tariq, wearing a gray suit, white shirt, maroon tie…and, God, he was beautiful. So beautiful…

"Your highness."

He smiled as he took her hand. "Surely we can dispense with such formality. Won't you address me as Tariq?"

"Tariq," she said, and wondered at the flutter of her pulse. He was very different today. Smiling, gracious, charming.

Very different, this man who was the father of her child, the source of the sperm that had entered her…

Color flooded her cheeks. Quickly she withdrew her hand and searched for something to say.

"Thank you for the flowers. They were beautiful."

"I'm glad you liked them. It was gracious of you to accept my apology."

"Well, I think—I think we both were in shock yesterday."

"I agree." The plane's engines had started; she could feel it moving. Tariq cupped her elbow. "Let's sit down, shall we?"

He led her to the table, waited until she'd settled into one of the chairs.

"This is—this is lovely."

"I've asked Yusuf to serve us once we're at flying altitude but perhaps you'd like something to drink? Fruit juice? Water? Tea?"

"Nothing, thank you."

The plane was still moving. Madison glanced out the window. They had turned onto a runway. Without warning, the little rush of apprehension came again.

"You know—you know, your highness—"

"Tariq."

"Yes, of course. Tariq. I've been thinking about this lunch—"

"You're thinking you should have said 'no.'"

Madison looked at him. No smile, this time. No expression at all. A fist seemed to close around her heart but then his mouth curved in a smile.

"I'm glad you didn't," he said softly. "This way, we can talk as long as we like and have the chance to get to know each other."

"The flight to Boston's less than an hour," she said with an answering smile.

"I promise you, Madison, we'll have all the time we need. Now, let's have lunch."

Iced Perrier, in crystal goblets. A clear broth. Scallops sautéed with asparagus. Blackberries and clotted cream. Mint tea for her, black coffee for him.

For him. For Tariq.

He was charming. Attentive. He was the man she'd met at the party, not the coldly contemptuous one who'd all but forced his way into her apartment last night.

And yet—and yet, something wasn't right. Something hovered just beneath the sophisticated polish. Something dark and dangerous and yes, incredibly exciting, and why would he have felt it necessary to freeze his seed...

"What are you thinking?"

His voice was low and rough. Madison felt her face heat. She shook her head in denial.

"I wasn't thinking anything in partic—"

"You were thinking, why did he arrange to give his sperm to FutureBorn?"

It was the topic they'd been discussing for two days now. Why blush over the words? But she wasn't; she was blushing at the image, the hot, sexy image...

"You are entitled to an answer, Madison, and it is as I told you. I am the heir to the throne of my country. It was not always so—my brother was older by two years, and he would have become sultan on our father's death." A muscle knotted in his jaw; he raised a hand imperiously and Yusuf hurried to clear the table, then disappear into the galley. "But Sharif lost his life in an accident. He had not yet married...he left no heir."

"And you? Why didn't you marry?"

"I hadn't wanted to," Tariq said bluntly. "Not then...but

Sharif's death changed everything. I began searching for a wife." He gave a mirthless laugh. "Believe me, I tried. It just didn't happen. Too much pressure, perhaps, or perhaps the Karma's been wrong. Whatever the reason, time was passing and I still had not taken a wife."

"Yes, but you're young."

"Fate is no respecter of age," he said quietly. "What happened to Sharif proved it. I kept thinking, what if something happened to me?" His eyes met hers. "Then I saw that program about FutureBorn."

"The program I was on?"

He nodded. "At first, I saw only your beauty. And then I met you and—"

"I—I don't want to talk about that night. It was a mistake."

"The only mistake," Tariq said huskily, "was letting you go."

"No. It was the right thing to do. I didn't want to get involved. I want…I want my own life. A career. A child."

"But not a husband."

"No."

"A child needs a father."

"Your highness. Tariq—"

"Let me be more explicit. My child needs a father."

Madison felt the warning tingle again. "Look, I came here in good faith. You said we'd talk—"

"We are." He rose, took her hand and drew her to her feet. "This child belongs to us both."

"No. Yes." God, he was confusing her. He was standing too close; she had to tip her head back to see his eyes and it made her dizzy, or maybe it was just his presence that made her dizzy. "We created this life, but I wanted it."

"So did I," he said grimly. "The only difference is, I wanted to choose my child's mother."

"I understand that. And I can't change what happened but I'm willing to grant you certain rights."

His lips drew back. Was that really supposed to be a smile?

"Will you, indeed, *habiba*?"

"You can visit six times a year."

"How generous."

His tone was flat. Madison wanted to step back but his hands were holding her elbows; she was trapped.

"You know, I don't have to give you that many visits. I don't have to give you *any* visits. So be grateful that I—"

"Grateful?" he said in a low growl.

"All right. That wasn't quite the way to put it but—"

"Have you heard nothing I said? The child you carry, *my* child, will be heir to the throne of Dubaac."

"That's ridiculous!"

"I am tired of arguing over something that is indisputable, Madison. I offered you a way out last night. Now, I offer it again. I will take you as my wife."

"That's it! Tell your pilot to turn this plane around. I am not going to Boston. I am not going anywhere. I am not going to have a conversation with a—a crazy man!"

"Is that what I am?" His hands clamped harder on her elbows; he lifted her to her toes. "Is that what you think when you feel my hands on your breasts and my tongue in your mouth?"

Her cheeks turned scarlet.

"You're despicable! Turn this plane around right now."

"It's too late for that."

"Then, as soon as we touch down in Boston, your pilot is to turn straight around and fly me home. Do you hear me, Tariq? I demand he return me to New York!"

"You are in no position to demand anything."

What a fool she'd been to agree to this lunch! Frantic,

Madison twisted against Tariq's hands. He laughed, pulled her closer and brought her tightly against his long, hard body.

"Breaking bread is an old custom of my people, *habiba*. It is one of the ways enemies become friends."

"You and I will never be friends. I despise you! To think that I—that I received sperm from you—"

"You mean, from a test tube." Cupping her face, he lifted it to him. His gaze swept over her, lingered on her lips. "From cold glass instead of warm flesh," he whispered. "On a physician's examining table instead of on a bed, with my arms around you, your legs around my waist, your mouth hot and wet under mine…"

"No," Madison cried, but he was already kissing her, kissing her without mercy until her head fell back…

Until the hands she'd raised to push him away instead curled into the thick, silky hair on the back of his head.

A sigh of surrender whispered from her throat; her lips parted in eager welcome to the thrust of his tongue.

Tariq swept her up into his arms, carried her through the cabin to a doorway in the rear of the plane.

But it was Madison who reached back and shut the door, locking them into the silken silence of his in-flight bedroom.

"Tariq," she whispered, "Tariq…"

His fingers fumbled at the buttons on her white silk blouse until he cursed and tore it open. She had worn no bra; she'd told herself it was a warm day but now, with his mouth closing around her nipple, with her cry of passion in the air, she knew she had worn none because of this, because she'd wanted this, ached for this.

For him. Only for him.

"Madison."

His voice was thick, hoarse with desire.

"Yes," whispered, "yes, yes…"

They tumbled onto the bed together. She lifted her hips and he pulled her skirt off; she reached for his zipper but his hands were there first and then, God, then he was free of his trousers and he was big, so big that for an instant, she was afraid…

"Touch me," he growled.

He took her hand and put it on his erect flesh. He pulsed with life beneath her fingers. And yes, she was right, he was enormous. She couldn't close her hand around him.

"Watch," he said thickly, and he moved forward, put his hands under her bottom. Lifted her. Entered her. Entered her on one long, exquisite thrust and she sobbed his name, cried out in ecstasy at the feel of him stretching her, filling her…

He bent to her, kissed her deeply, hungrily. She put her arms around him; she could feel the fine tension in him, his muscles quivering under her hands as he held back, gave her body time to adjust to his size.

But waiting was more than she could bear. She moved. Moved again.

"*Habiba*," he said in a warning whisper.

"Yes," she said, rising to him as he began to move, as she found his rhythm and matched it…

And came, a heartbeat later, came on an endless, undulating wave of passion as he groaned, threw his head back, buried himself even deeper within her and exploded inside her.

He fell against her, his face in the crook of her shoulder. His breathing was heavy; his weight bore her down into the bed but she loved it, the feel of his body against hers, the scent of him, clean sweat and hard sex and all of it gloriously male…

All of it for a purpose.

The final vestiges of passion ebbed away. Cold reality set in.

God, what had she done?

He had taken her only to weaken her. To prove how fragile her resolve was in the face of his power. He was a man who always got what he wanted....

And what he wanted was her baby.

"Get off me!" Her voice was low, as broken as she felt. When he didn't move, she banged her fists against his shoulders. "Damn you, get off!"

Tariq stirred. He lifted his head, rolled to his side and put his arm across her, hand cupping her naked hip and keeping her where he wanted her.

"Such charming pillow talk, *habiba*." His tone was lazy; his gaze hooded. "Are you always this sweet-tempered after sex?"

She didn't answer and he took his time looking at her. She was more beautiful than ever, with her blond hair wild against the pillows, her mouth and nipples rosy from his kisses, her breasts flushed from her climax.

The only thing that spoiled it was the look in her eyes. She had given herself to him and now she hated herself for it.

It wasn't as if he'd planned to do things this way.

Kidnapping her? Yes. Taking her to Dubaac, to the Golden Palace? Yes, again. There, he'd imagined seducing her with cold deliberation.

But this—the hot, overpowering passion that had all but consumed him. The soul-deep hunger. The need to have her, to possess her...

He had not anticipated any of it, or how badly he wanted to take her in his arms now and kiss her, change the expression on her face to what it had been moments ago—a mix of desire and need and something that transcended submission...

Tariq rolled to the edge of the bed, got to his feet and zipped up his trousers.

"What's the matter, *habiba*? Have you never been played a game and been defeated before?"

Madison grabbed at the duvet and dragged it to her throat as she scrambled up against the pillows.

"Is that what this is to you? A game?"

"What else could it be? A game, of course, and one you play so well. The temptress and the toad. The temptress and the prince." His smile hardened. "But you're right. This is no time for games. All that concerns me is my child."

Tears stung Madison's eyes. Her pride was shattered. Her clothing was ruined. Once she stepped out of this room, everyone on the plane, his obedient, heel-clicking minions, would know what they had done.

"I was right about you," she said brokenly. "You're a horrible human being! All this, just to—to get me into your bed…"

"You underestimate me, Madison."

"What do you mean?"

"How long do you think it takes to fly to Boston?"

The change in topic caught her off-guard. She stared at him. He could almost see her coming up with the correct answer, then calculating how long they'd actually been in the air.

"That's right," he said softly. "We've been flying almost three hours."

"Then why…then why haven't we landed yet?"

He moved swiftly, grasping her shoulders, bringing her to her knees in the center of the bed. The duvet fell away, leaving her naked and exposed to his eyes.

"Do you know anything about my country, *habiba*?" He smiled; the look on her face was all the answer he required. "In some ways, we are very modern. In others, we still cling to the past."

"That's fascinating," she said, trying to control the tremor in her voice, "but—"

"For instance, a man who wishes to take an unwilling woman as his bride may still resort to the old ways. He carries her off, takes her to his bed and she is his forever."

He saw the color drain from her face.

"That's ridiculous. It's barbaric. It's—it's a joke."

"No joke, sweetheart. There is more to the world than America."

"Are you trying to scare me? Because it won't work, your highness. Luckily for me, this *is* America, not Dubaac!"

He caught her face between his hands and kissed her, hard, again and again until he felt the first softening of her mouth under his.

The knowledge that she still wanted him, despite everything, made him want to push her back against the pillows and take her again and again until she was clinging to him, whispering to him, until his possession was all that mattered.

But he was not a fool.

She knew how to use her sexuality, and he knew better than to succumb to it.

So he drew back, ran his thumbs over the razor-sharp bones of her cheeks and smiled into her eyes.

"We are over the Atlantic, *habiba*. And though I am sure you find my title an amusing anachronism I assure you, it is quite real. It has power. For instance, it means that this plane is the equivalent of Dubaacian soil."

Her eyes widened; he smiled.

"That's right, *habiba*. For all intents and purposes, you are already in Dubaac. And, because of what just happened in my bed, you are now my wife."

He let go of her so suddenly that she tumbled back against the pillows.

"And I," he said, his smile gone, his eyes flat as glass, "am your lord and master."

CHAPTER SEVEN

MADISON stared at the door Tariq had shut behind him.

Shut. Not slammed. A display of hot anger would have been frightening. His icy calmness was terrifying.

She flew to the door and locked it even though she knew it was an empty gesture. A lock would not keep him out. This was his plane, staffed by people loyal to a prince who thought he lived in an earlier century.

That he had brought her on board, carried her to his bed, kept her in it while he forced himself on her...

She bit back a moan.

Tariq hadn't forced himself on her. She had responded to each touch, each kiss, urged him to do more, to take her and take her and take her...

No. She wasn't going there. Her moment of weakness was in the past. She'd had sex with him. It wasn't the end of the world. She was almost thirty, she was not a virgin; she'd had sex before.

But never like that.

Never so she wouldn't have noticed if the world had ended as long as Tariq held her, moved deep, deep inside her...

Madison spun away from the door.

What he had done had been a pure, masculine flaunting of

power. What *she* had done was disgrace herself, but reliving what had happened was pointless. Thinking about that—that nasty fairy tale he'd told her about kidnapped women and forced marriages, was pointless, too.

It had to be a lie.

Not even the Prince from Hell would think he could get away with that kind of thing.

He'd tried to scare her and he'd succeeded, but she was past that now. What mattered was getting through the next hours, until he wearied of this new game. That meant getting dressed, leaving this room and facing him with her head high.

First, she needed to clean up. She could smell his scent on her skin.

There was another door in the room. Did it open onto a bathroom? Yes. A bathroom, complete with a shower stall. She turned the water on full, stepped under it, reached for the soap...

His soap.

This same bar had slid over his body, over all those hard muscles, over the steel-in-silk part of him that had filled her...

Madison caught her breath.

She waited, let the water beat down on her bowed head. Then she got busy scrubbing and rinsing.

She dried off. Finger-combed her hair. Stepped back into the bedroom, flung open the drawers of a built-in dresser and found shirts and jeans. His clothing, of course, and she hated the thought of it against her skin but what choice did she have?

She dressed quickly, rolling up the legs of a pair of faded jeans, securing the waist with a belt she dragged through the loops and knotted. She plucked a shirt from the drawer, cotton so soft it might have been silk. The fit was a bad joke but she managed, folding back the sleeves, gathering the tails together and tying them just above the jeans.

Then she went back into the bathroom and stared at herself in the mirror.

A dressed-for-success vice president had boarded this plane.

The woman looking back at her now was a mess.

No makeup. Her hair was drying in wavy tendrils, the way it always did if she didn't blow it dry. She looked ridiculous in Tariq's clothing and there was no way his crew would not know why she was wearing it but hadn't she just finished telling herself that they'd know, anyway, and that she didn't give a damn?

All that mattered was finding out what he was up to because surely, he would not take her out of the States. He wasn't a fool. Prince or no prince, she would bring charges against him.

He had to realize that.

Madison hesitated, hand on the knob. A deep breath. A slow exhalation. Then she unlocked the door and stepped into the cabin.

Someone had dimmed the lights, though a bright spotlight illuminated Tariq, who was seated on a leather love seat. A tall, ice-filled glass was on the table next to him; an open portable computer was in his lap.

He looked calm and contained, every dark hair in place, his clothes neat and unruffled.

Why did that made her angry?

"Tariq."

He looked up, saw her, let his eyes sweep over her. She could read nothing whatsoever in his face. Her temper, already at a simmer, began to boil.

"I see you found something to wear."

Madison raised her chin. "Not the latest in fashion, but it will have to do."

"I also see that we're finally on a first name basis."

"I want an explanation."

"Do you?" A slow smile softened his mouth. "I'll be happy to oblige, *habiba*, though I would have thought what happened in my bed was clear enough."

He was trying to embarrass her. And he was succeeding—but she'd be damned if she'd let him know it.

God, what a horrible man!

"How long before we're home?"

"Sit down, Madison."

"Answer the question."

His eyes narrowed. "Try asking it with some courtesy and perhaps I will."

"I want to know how long it's going to take until—"

"Six hours."

She blinked. "Six…?"

"We've been flying for four hours. Six more, and we arrive in Dubaac."

"I said, home. New York. If you think you can frighten me by pretending we're—"

"Why would I want to frighten you, *habiba*? My home is Dubaac. That is where we are going."

"You mean—you mean, when you said—when you said—"

Tariq shot to his feet.

Crimson patches had ridden high on her cheeks when she'd finally emerged from his bedroom. Now, she'd lost color so quickly he was afraid she might faint, and he'd already been the cause of that once before.

He wasn't going to let it happen again.

Bad enough he'd made love to her without asking if it was safe for the baby. At least, then, he'd had an excuse. The part of his anatomy that had been doing his thinking wasn't much for logic.

But he could have dealt with what she'd just asked him with a little more finesse.

It was only that she drove him insane when she got that holier-than-thou look on her beautiful face…

"Sit!" he barked, and before she could protest, he caught her in the curve of his arm and drew her down on the love seat with him. "Are you going to pass out?"

"No," she whispered.

No, indeed, he thought grimly.

"Put your head forward."

"I'm fine."

"Did I ask your opinion, *habiba*? Bend forward. Lean against me."

She wanted to argue or, better still, ignore the command, but his hand was on the back of her head, gently but insistently easing it forward. With a sigh, she let her forehead settle against his shoulder.

The terrible truth was that she did feel woozy. The doctor had said her health was excellent but that in early pregnancy some women might feel that way…

"Ahh," she said, and shut her eyes at the wonderfully cold sting of ice against the nape of her neck.

"Good?"

She nodded. Wonderful, was more like it, but why tell him that?

"Is it—is it the child? Are you—"

"No. It's nothing like that. The baby's okay."

"Perhaps we should not have…" He hesitated; his voice lowered and she felt the warmth of his breath at her temple. "Perhaps we should not have made love."

Madison looked up. "What we did," she said, "was have sex."

"Lean your head against me, damn it!" The ice cube

moved lightly over her skin again. "Perhaps you should eat something."

"We just had lunch…"

"Hours ago," he said sternly. "Besides, you are eating for two now, remember? Yusuf!"

Yusuf came running, as if conjured by Aladdin's lamp.

"My lord?"

"Bring us something to drink. Water. Juice. Something cold."

"Certainly, your highness."

Yusuf inclined his head and started toward the galley. Tariq's bellow stopped him.

"Sir?"

"Bring something sweet, as well. Cake. Chocolate."

"Of course, your highness."

"And do it quickly!"

"I will, sir."

Madison, face still tucked against Tariq's shoulder, gave a little laugh.

"Doesn't he know that dawdlers can be drawn and quartered?"

"Very amusing. Do you feel better?"

"Yes. I can get up now."

"You cannot." She heard the cube of ice plop back into the glass. "What you may do is lift your head. Slowly. Good." His arm tightened around her. "Sit still and take deep breaths."

"Are the words 'please' and 'thank you' not part of your vocabulary?"

"Excuse me?"

"I said—"

"I heard what you said."

Yusuf appeared with a tray. Tariq took a tall glass of iced orange juice from it and held it to Madison's lips. "Drink."

"Oh, for pity's sake, I'm pregnant, not—" Her eyes lifted to Yusuf's, whose face was a perfect blank. "I'm pregnant," she hissed to Tariq, "not sick. I don't need you to hold the glass for me."

Tariq frowned but he handed her the glass, then watched carefully as she drained it.

"Thank you."

"You are welcome."

"I was speaking to Yusuf." Deliberately, Madison smiled at the attendant, who looked horrified as he took the glass from her and scurried off.

Tariq glared at Madison.

"Do you think you will win allies by insulting me?"

"When are you taking me home?"

"I asked you a question."

"Answer mine first."

By Ishtar, the woman was impossible! Had she no sense of propriety? They would have to discuss her behavior, and soon.

"Not until you tell me if you feel all right."

"I already told you that I did."

"That's not what I mean." A muscle knotted in his jaw. "Before. What we did…" Damn it, he was stumbling all over his words. "When we made love. Did I hurt you?"

"I told you. We didn't make love, we had—"

"Madison. Please. Did I hurt you?"

Please? That was a first. She thought about lying, but to what end? "No," she said, "you didn't."

"Good. Because I—I did not think…"

"It's too late to apologize."

His eyes narrowed; he caught her chin and turned her face to him.

"I am not apologizing. A man would be a fool to apologize

for what happened in that bed." He paused. "But I should have considered your condition. I should have thought of the child."

"The baby."

"That's what I said."

"You said 'the child.' You always say 'the child,' except when you call my baby your heir."

"I'm not trying to quarrel with you, Madison. I only asked if the child—the baby—is all right."

"My baby's fine." Her cheeks bloomed with color. "Sex won't hurt it, not even the kind a man forces on a woman."

"Is lying and pretending you didn't want what happened the way you make peace with yourself for crying out in my arms?" he said, his voice rough.

"You forced me into this situation. If you hadn't—"

"We would have ended up in bed eventually."

"That's a lie!"

"It's the truth and you know it. We wanted each other from the beginning. That I ended up spending my seed in your womb by means of a syringe instead of as nature intended was a quirk of fate."

Madison stared at him. His eyes had gone that shade of silver she knew meant he was aroused. And, incredibly, so was she.

How could talking about a sexless act be so sexy?

And how could he have taken the conversation so far from where it belonged?

"I don't know why we're talking about this. The only thing I want to discuss is—"

"I took the liberty of preparing some things besides chocolate and cake, your highness." Yusuf paused beside them with a wheeled cart. "Shall I—"

Tariq waved his hand. "We will serve ourselves."

The attendant inclined his head and left them. Tariq uncovered platters of cakes and cookies, a selection of cheeses, crusty bread, fruits and chocolates. Everything looked and smelled delicious.

Tariq filled a plate and put it in front of her.

"Eat," he commanded.

She thought of saying no. Of telling him she was not one of his servants, trained to sit and stay on cue but her stomach gave an unladylike growl. Tariq laughed, she shot him a cold look, and dug in.

She emptied her plate, drank more iced orange juice and just when she looked wistfully at the coffee in Tariq's cup, Yusuf appeared with a pot of mint tea.

"Thank you," she said, and was rewarded with a blush.

"You are welcome, my lady."

"Princess."

Both Yusuf and Madison looked at Tariq. He smiled as he reached for her hand, though his eyes flashed a warning.

"The lady has done me the honor of becoming my wife."

"No," Madison said sharply, and winced as his hand tightened almost painfully on hers.

"My wife wished to keep our news secret as long as possible," he said, raising her hand to his lips, "but since we will land in my country—her new country—in another few hours, I thought it was time to announce our news. You, Yusuf, are the first to know."

Yusuf beamed at them both. "It is wonderful news, sir, and I am honored you shared it with me. May you have a long and happy life."

"Thank you." Tariq smiled. "And now, if you would give us privacy for the rest of the flight…"

Madison controlled her temper until they were alone. Then she tore her hand from Tariq's and shot to her feet.

"You can tell all the ridiculous lies you like—"

"It was no lie," he said calmly. "Or have you already forgotten what I said about an old custom of my people?"

"It is not a custom of *my* people! It is not a custom anywhere in the civilized world!"

"Watch what you say to me, wife."

"Do not call me that! Just because you have some—some barbaric bit of folklore that must make anthropologists shriek with joy doesn't mean that I—"

Tariq was on his feet, his hands cupping her shoulders before she could finish the sentence.

"You will not take that tone with me!"

"You tell your—your slave that I'm married to you and all you're worried about is how I sound when I talk to you? I don't know if you're just thickheaded or so out of touch with reality that you—"

He kissed her. It was either that or silence her some other way and he had never been a man to use violence on a woman…

Besides, he loved her taste.

She struggled. He cupped her face, held her captive to his kiss, felt a rush of fierce joy when her lips softened and he felt the first sign of her sweet, eager response.

"Hate me all you like," he said hoarsely, "but you will obey me. You will respect me." His eyes darkened. "And when I take you to bed, you will answer my passion with your own because it is what you want, *habiba,* it is what you shall always want, even as you hate me with all your heart."

He kissed her again and as she melted against him, the stirring of an emotion far more dangerous than desire coursed through his blood.

It stopped him for an instant, but Madison moved against him and he forgot everything but wanting her.

He swept her into his arms, carried her through the cabin and into the bedroom, shouldered the door closed and came down on the bed with his wife in his arms.

"I do hate you," she whispered, but her arms held him tight as she brought his head down to hers for another kiss.

His blood thundered, but he forced himself to go slowly, to undo the buttons of her shirt, the zipper of her jeans.

His shirt.

His jeans.

Could she possibly know how sexy she'd looked, wearing them?

He spread the shirt open, kissed her breasts, loving their silken texture, the sweet taste of her nipples. He slid his hand down the back of her jeans, slipped his fingers between her thighs and stroked the tender, weeping flower he found there.

Madison cried out.

He caught the cry with his mouth and fought to hang on to his sanity.

"Please," she whispered, tugging at his shirt, and he pulled back, stripped it off, groaned as he felt her hands on him, exploring him, stroking over his chest, his shoulders, moving down his ridged abdomen. And when she found him, cupped her hand over the taut denim, Tariq gritted his teeth, gave in to the exquisite pleasure for a heartbeat and then caught her wrists and brought them to her sides before it was too late.

Carefully he gathered his wife to him. She was trembling and he was aroused beyond anything he had ever experienced, but he knew that to take her again would be wrong.

She was pregnant. She was exhausted. She was torn between hating him and wanting him...

And he—he needed something more from her than sex, something that had no name.

The room was dark. The air was cool. He drew up the duvet, eased Madison's head to his shoulder. Her breath sighed against his skin as he lay his hand gently over the place in her body where the child—where *their* child—lay dreaming.

"Go to sleep, *habiba*," he said softly.

She bristled, as he should have known she would.

"Do *not* tell me what to do, Tariq! I am not the least bit—"

She yawned. He smiled. A second later, she was asleep.

CHAPTER EIGHT

MADISON awoke with a start.

She lay in a canopied bed the size of a football field in a vast, high-ceilinged room. Sheer curtains that diffused the sunlight pouring through a wall of glass.

The bed linens were soft and cool against her skin.

Her naked skin.

She shot up against the pillows, clutching the bedcovers to her breasts. *Where am I?* she thought and even in that moment of terrifying disorientation, she wanted to laugh at the pathetic cliché.

Except, it wasn't a cliché, it was the truth.

Her memories of the night were fragments of a dream. The last thing she recalled with any clarity was Tariq carrying her to bed on his plane, undressing her, caressing her, holding her in his arms…

Madison closed her eyes.

Had she really fallen asleep that way? In his arms? Her head on his bare shoulder, his breath warm against her temple?

And after that, what? Everything was murky. The plane, landing. Tariq, wrapping her in a quilt, carrying her to an SUV that sped along a road under a sky shot through with silver…

"Madame?"

Madison's eyes flew open. A woman stood in the open doorway, a tentative smile on her lips.

"Forgive me, my lady. I knocked, but there was no answer."

"No." Madison forced an answering smile. "No, that's all right. Who are you?"

"I am Sahar. Your servant."

Her servant? What did you say to that?

"I have brought you mint tea."

"Mint tea," Madison said brightly. "That's—that's excellent."

"Do you wish it in bed, or shall I put it near the windows?"

"Oh. Ah, by the windows will be..." Madison took a deep breath. "Sahar?"

"My lady?"

"Where—exactly where am I?" The woman's eyebrows shot toward her hairline. "I mean," Madison said quickly, "what is the name of this place?"

Sahar looked at her. Madison figured the expression on her face was pretty much the same expression that had been on *her* face the time a befuddled tourist had asked her where the Empire State building was while standing directly in front of it.

"It is the Golden Palace, of course."

The Golden Palace. "Of course," Madison said. "And, ah, and the city is...?"

Sahar's expression went from bemused to alarmed.

"We are in the city of Dubaac, my lady."

"Right. Dubaac. The city. In the country of—"

"The city, the country are one," a male voice said. Tariq strolled into the room and waved his hand in dismissal. "That will be all, Sahar."

The servant bowed and scuttled out the door. Tariq closed it, then leaned back against it, arms folded. Madison's heart banged against her ribs. He looked different. Taller, somehow.

More imposing, if that were possible. And—and, yes, beautiful in a cream-colored shirt, faded jeans and riding boots.

"Good morning, *habiba*. Did you sleep well?"

"Do you care?"

He grinned. "I can see we're off to a fine start."

"We are off to no start."

"Meaning?"

"Meaning, you are not welcome in this room, Tariq—and where are my clothes?"

His smile tilted. "Don't you really mean, 'Who undressed me and put me to bed?'"

Why did he always manage to make her blush? "An excellent question but then, I have a lot of excellent questions. And I'm not asking them until I am out of bed and dressed."

"No one's stopping you."

"You are."

"A little late to worry about modesty," he said, his voice silken, "don't you think?"

"Damn it, Tariq…"

"Sahar undressed you and put you to bed."

He could see it wasn't the answer she'd expected. Her face, lovely in the bright light of morning, was a study in surprise.

"It would have been improper for me to have done so."

"But—but I thought—I mean, if you and I are—if we really are—"

"Husband and wife, *habiba*, are the words you're searching for."

"Don't play games with me."

He had wondered how she would be this morning. Subdued, he had told himself and told himself, too, that he hoped that would be the case because it would make everything that came next easier.

But his wife was not subdued. Frightened, yes. The tremor in her voice gave it away, but she was facing him as she always did, chin high, eyes steady. A tiger ready to do battle even though he had turned her life upside down, stolen her away from everything familiar, forced her into his bed…

Tariq's throat went dry.

Except, he hadn't forced her. She had gone willingly, moved beneath him eagerly, matched him kiss for kiss, touch for touch.

Damn it!

He swung away, shocked by the swift response of his body, angered by it. He strode into the dressing room, determined not to let her see the evidence of her power over him, and returned with a long silk robe that he tossed on the bed.

"Get up," he said harshly, "and make yourself presentable."

"Presentable? How? I have nothing to—"

"There are clothes for you in the dressing room."

"Clothes for the last woman you kidnapped and brought here?"

His jaw tightened. Did she really think he would indulge her in debate…or tell her he had never brought a woman here, to the Golden Palace? There was no need for her to know that.

As it was, he had enough to tell her—and to prepare her to accept.

"Select something appropriate," he said coldly. "Then we will have coffee and talk."

"Appropriate for what?"

He looked at her, sitting up in his bed, against his pillows, holding the silk robe over her breasts.

Her skin would feel as soft as the robe.

It would slide over her nipples, turning them into tight little buds. He could still recall their taste. Sweet. Cool.

Delicate. And the scent of her skin, just there. Like wildflowers on a June morning…

Was he insane?

They were minutes away from facing his father, from gaining the approval he had not yet told her their union would require, and he was turning as hard as a schoolboy staring at his first centerfold.

It made him even more angry. It was her fault. Surely it could not be his!

"I asked you a question, Tariq. Appropriate for what?"

Her mouth was trembling. He wanted to go to her. Take her in his arms. Tell her—tell her—

"And I told you to get up," he snapped. "Learn to do as you are told and things will go easier for you. And before you bother telling me that you hate me… Hatred is always the prerogative of a wife."

She snarled a word at him. He ignored it, turned his back, folded his arms and let his damnable imagination take over as he heard the whisper of silk, the pad of bare feet, the hiss of the shower running in the en suite bathroom.

And groaned.

Why was he standing here when he could strip off his clothes, go to her, step under the water and take her in his arms?

She would protest, because she hated him. But hating him didn't keep her from wanting him and once he touched her, drew her naked body back against his so she could feel the urgency of his desire, she would sigh his name, let her head droop against his shoulder as he cupped her breasts, as he slid his hands down her body in the most intimate of caresses.

Then he would turn her toward him, she would raise her mouth to his, wind her arms around his neck and he would cup her bottom, lift her to him, feel her legs wrap around his hips as he thrust deep, deep into her heat...

Tariq groaned again. He was a man in the sweetest kind of pain.

She was killing him, this woman he had not wanted in his life. Killing him—and his sanity depended on concentrating on the long nights he would spend, making her pay the penalty for it.

Madison stood under the shower, waiting.

She knew Tariq's game.

Any minute now, he'd open the bathroom door and step into the shower stall with her. As far as he was concerned, he could bark at her, order her around, then take her in his arms and dazzle her with his sexual expertise.

Well, it wasn't going to work this time.

It wasn't going to work at all, she realized as the minutes slid past, because it wasn't going to happen.

The door to the bedroom stayed shut.

She was alone, and he was going to leave her that way.

Good, she thought grimly. The last thing she wanted was him forcing himself on her again. Caressing her. Kissing her.

A little sound whispered from her lips. What was happening to her? She was changing into a woman she didn't know.

Too little sleep, that was the problem. That, and the change in time zones...

Madison frowned, lifted her face to the spray and blanked her mind to everything but survival.

The dressing room opened off the bath as well as the bedroom. It was the size of her Manhattan living room and filled with clothes. Acres of them. Trousers. Sweaters. Blouses. Dresses.

Gowns. Shoes. There was lingerie, too: delicate bras and thongs in soft shades of peach and palest blue, all surely handmade.

She selected a bra. A thong. A gorgeous pair of white cotton trousers and a white silk T-shirt.

Everything fit perfectly.

Her mouth thinned.

Tariq obviously preferred his women to be built as she was. Surely all these things, this suite, had been arranged by a prince for his mistress. For his mistresses.

Not that she gave a damn.

She dropped the towel, dressed quickly, slid her feet into a pair of exquisite white high-heeled sandals. The dressing room was mirrored; Madison glanced at her reflection, ran her hands through her still-damp hair, flung open the door and marched into the bedroom.

"Here I am," she said briskly, "appropriately dressed or—"

But the room was empty.

Tariq had drawn back the gauzy curtains, revealing a door in the wall of glass. He stood on a stone balcony beside a table set for breakfast, sipping from a cup as he looked out over a turquoise sea.

Madison's breath caught.

How beautiful this place was. How beautiful Tariq was.

If only he'd brought her here because he wanted her. Because he needed her. Because she was someone he cared for instead of his virtual captive.

Did he sense her presence? He must have because he swung toward her, his gray gaze sweeping from the top of her head to her toes and then back up again.

She thought her heart would stop at the sudden glint in his eyes.

"You look…" He cleared his throat. "You look beautiful, *habiba.*"

She came within a breath of saying he did, too, before she regained her senses.

"I'm so glad you approve," she said, frost clinging to every word.

"Come," he said, motioning to the table. "Sit with me and have breakfast."

The word made her salivate. "I'm not hungry," she lied. "And I'm not Sahar. I don't take orders from you."

His gaze flew over her again. "No," he said softly, "you are not." Smiling, he held out his hand. "Join me. Please."

She wondered how much the simple word had cost him. Enough to make doing as he'd asked worthwhile? She decided it was, if only because not eating was foolish and she knew she'd need all her wits about her to make him stop toying with her.

She ignored his outstretched hand, pulled out a chair for herself and sat down at the table. Tariq shrugged and sat down across from her. She'd half expected him to clap his hands or press a buzzer that would bring Sahar running. Instead he poured her juice, served her crepes with crème fraiche and tiny raspberries, and filled her cup with tea.

She was almost painfully aware of him watching her as she ate. Finally he cleared his throat.

"Good?"

She thought of lying, but what was the point?

"Yes."

"And you feel well? The baby—"

"The baby's fine. So am I—unless you count the fact that I'm angry as hell!" She put down her fork, touched her mouth with her linen napkin and decided there'd never be a better time than right now. "Tariq. I want this nonsense to end."

His eyes narrowed. "Nonsense?"

"Nonsense. You know. The flight here. This—this little sojourn at—at—"

"The Golden Palace."

"Whatever. I've had enough. I want to go home."

"You are home," he said evenly. "I thought you understood that."

"You said what—what you'd done made me your wife."

"Carrying you off? Making love to you?"

She felt her face heat. "Stealing me," she said. "And then—and then taking me."

A little smile, quick and sexy, slanted across his mouth. "I may have stolen you, *habiba,* but I did not 'take' you. We made love."

"I'm not going to debate it. The fact is, you said those things made me your wife."

"They did."

Madison took a deep breath, held it for an instant, then let it out.

"And yet, this morning you said it would not have been proper for you to have put me to bed last night. Or to have shared that bed with me."

"Believe me, *habiba*," he said, his voice low and a little rough, "I regret not having been able to do those things as much as you do."

"I don't regret them! That's not my point at all!"

"Then, what is your point, Madison?"

"If you'd told the truth, if I really were your wife—"

"You are." Tariq tossed his napkin on the table and rose to his feet. "But I want my father's recognition of that fact. His formal recognition."

"How touching."

His face darkened. "You would make a joke of it. I assure you, this is not a joking matter. My child—"

"*My* child."

"*Our* child," he said coldly, "will someday inherit the throne of an ancient and honorable kingdom. For the sake of his future, for the sake of my people's future, our union must have the royal blessing."

"My son speaks the truth, young woman. My approval is vital to the future of Dubaac."

Madison shot to her feet. A small man, white-haired and stooped, stood in the doorway. Tariq, looking startled, hurried toward him.

"Father. I did not expect—"

"No. Obviously not." The sultan, his expression unreadable, looked at Madison. "And this is your wife."

"Yes, Father. I told the prime minister I would bring her to you at noon."

"Did you expect me to wait that long to see the woman who carries my grandchild?" The sultan frowned. "She could use more meat on her bones."

"I agree, Father, and—"

"Excuse me," Madison said with defiance, though her heart was pounding like a drum. "I do not need more meat on my bones, I do not like being spoken of as if I were not present and I am not your son's wife."

The sultan's expression eased. "She is exactly as you said, Tariq." His eyebrows rose at Madison's look of surprise. "My son told me all about you."

She blinked. "He did?"

"Last night, after you and he arrived. And, I admit, I was not pleased."

An ally? Madison mentally crossed her fingers. "No. Of course you weren't. I mean, why would you be…"

"My son is a prince. He is my heir. His wedding should have been celebrated properly, by the joined Nations." The sultan's expression softened. "But he explained how you met and fell deeply in love."

Madison crossed her arms over her chest. "Did he, indeed?"

"And I understand." The old man's lips twitched. "I know you'd planned to seek my blessing but that fate and nature intervened. After all, I was young once. I remember how hot the blood can run."

"No," Madison said quickly, "that isn't—"

"Father." Tariq came to her side, slid his arm around her waist. It looked like a gesture of tenderness but his hand splayed over her hip as if it were made of steel. "You're embarrassing my bride."

"That's not true. I'm not—"

"Of course you are, *habiba*." Tariq's voice was soft but the look he flashed at her upturned face was a cold warning. "It's only natural that you'd feel our story is far too personal to share."

Madison blinked. Hadn't he told his father how this child had been conceived?

"As I said," the sultan continued, "I am human. I stayed awake all night, thinking." His voice went soft. "I decided to be happy for you and for my son, and especially for the baby he put in your womb, even if it was done a new way."

Tariq felt Madison's start of surprise. He tightened his arm around her.

"He means," he said carefully, "without us marrying first, *habiba*."

"In fact, I must admit I am delighted that you agreed to an

old-fashioned joining of your bodies, hearts and souls so that no one will dare call your baby illegitimate."

Madison ignored the pressure of Tariq's encircling arm. "Sir," she said, "you don't under—"

"There is no need to thank me, my dear. I love my son. I love my people. Why would I not be prepared to love the woman he loves, and the child she carries?" The sultan smiled. "Welcome to our family, Princess."

Madison stared at the eyes bright with hope but rheumy with age. What could she say that wouldn't take that hope from the old man? If she told him the truth, that she hadn't agreed to anything, that she wanted to leave this place and Tariq, she'd probably break his heart.

No. She couldn't do that. Tariq had created this mess. Let him be the one to fix it, not she.

The sultan held out his arms. Madison fixed a smile to her lips and walked into his embrace. He kissed each of her cheeks, then held her at arm's length and chuckled.

"Such a nice surprise my son brings me." His smile tilted. "Did Tariq tell you of the death of his brother?"

"Yes. I mean, he said something about—"

"I am happy for the first time since that terrible day. A lovely woman, with my first grandchild in her womb… Who would have thought a tragedy could leave a man twice blessed?"

Color flooded Madison's face. Tariq saw it and knew she was not blushing at the compliment but at the depth of their lie.

He felt something knife into his heart.

His bride had honor. She had integrity. Where was his?

"Tonight," the sultan said briskly, "we shall celebrate. I have contacted all our friends and family. It is short notice but they assure me they will all be here to share our good fortune

and to hear you announce your marriage and make it official."
He smiled. "My son, you have done well."

A muscle flickered in Tariq's jaw. "Father. Just a minute.
I must talk to you—"

"We'll have time to talk tomorrow." The old man let go of
Madison and clasped Tariq's shoulders. "You have done a
good thing," he said quietly, "a fine thing. Your brother can
rest easy. Wherever his spirit dwells, I am sure he is as proud
of you as I."

The sultan embraced Tariq, kissed Madison again and
retraced his steps into the house.

Tariq stood motionless.

The scene had gone exactly as he'd hoped.

And he despised himself for it.

His father was wrong. Sharif would *not* be proud of him.
No one would. He had drawn them all into a monstrous lie.
His father, his people, his dead brother and, most of all, the
woman who carried his child… He had dishonored all of them.

It was not difficult to see that he had dishonored his unborn
child, too.

"Tariq?"

He felt Madison's hand fall lightly on his shoulder. He
ached for her touch, for her absolution, but he knew damned
well he didn't deserve it so he swung toward her and caught
hold of her wrists.

"I was wrong," he said harshly. "About everything. I got
so caught up in the need for an heir that I was blind to everything else. And—and I forgot a simple thing called honor."

Madison stared at the stranger who was her husband.
Moments ago, all she'd wanted was to finish this awful
charade. Then, she'd met an old man fighting the ravages of
time, the loss of a son and the burden of leadership.

Looking at Tariq's drawn face, her heart constricted.

He had been born to awesome responsibility. He'd lost his brother and, from the looks of it, he would probably soon lose his father, too. In the face of all that, he had done what he had to do.

What any man of honor would do. How could she not have recognized that until now?

"*Habiba.* I have wronged you. And I—"

Madison shook her head. "You did what fate demanded."

"Sharif would not be proud of me."

"I think he would."

"I lied to my father, I forced you into marriage—"

"You loved your brother."

"With all my heart."

"And you love your father. You love your land and your people." She shook her head. "I didn't really understand."

"What is there to understand? I put myself ahead of everything. Ahead of you, our baby, even the righteousness of truth. And that is an unforgivable evil."

"You were worried," she said softly. "About the future of your people and your child."

"You're being generous, *habiba.* I didn't think of our baby, I thought of my heir."

"Maybe—but somewhere along the way, your heir became our baby." Her lips curved in a smile. "And look at what's just happened. You said you were wrong. You apologized. Tariq, this is a day to remember."

Tariq looked at his wife. How good she was, this woman whose life he had turned upside down. How could he have seen her only as a vessel for his needs?

He took a strand of her hair and let it curl around his finger, stalling for time even though he knew what he had to do.

"Madison. I'm going to take you home. To New York. We'll meet with my attorney and work out some sort of arrangement. I will, of course, support our child. I only ask that you let me share in its life and teach it to be proud of its heritage."

"You don't have to ask those things of me, Tariq. We're married."

Not yet, Tariq thought. He had announced the marriage to his flight staff, to his father, but until he stood before his people with Madison at his side…

"We are, aren't we, Tariq?"

He hesitated. She deserved the truth.

"Tariq. Are we married?"

Tariq looked at the impossible, difficult, untamable female who carried his child.

Her eyes were very dark; her breathing was quick. She was not what he had ever looked for. Except for her beauty, she had none of the traits he'd believed a wife should have.

And the thought of giving her up made his heart ache.

"If I were not a royal, we would be," he said softly. "But I am a prince, *habiba*. So until my father makes the announcement before our people—"

Madison put her fingers over his lips.

"I had no father, Tariq. I told myself that my child wouldn't need one, either. And then you appeared at my door. The anonymous donor who'd made me pregnant." Her eyes met his. "But you're not that anymore. You're a man. A good man. How can I deny your right to this child, or its right to you?" She swallowed dryly. "Let your father make the announcement tonight."

They looked at each other for a long moment. Then Tariq groaned and gathered her in his arms.

"You do me an incredible honor," he said softly. "I will be

a good husband. A good father. I swear it, *habiba*. I will do everything I can to make you happy. I swear that, too."

Madison nodded. She knew that he would...

But he would not love her. That was all right, wasn't it? Love wasn't part of this arrangement. Why would she want it to be? She didn't love this man. Certainly she didn't love—

"*Habiba*?"

Madison stopped thinking, rose to her husband and sealed their agreement with a kiss.

CHAPTER NINE

TARIQ said he would see her later, that he'd have to spend most of the day in meetings.

"Will you be all right, *habiba*?"

Madison had said yes, of course, she'd be fine. She was accustomed to being on her own; why would this be any different?

The answer came within seconds of his closing the door.

There was a phone beside the bed. Seeing it made her realize she hadn't contacted her office. Even if she'd had the time, her cell phone wasn't geared for overseas use.

All right. She'd call now. Her P.A. was probably frantic, trying to figure out what had happened to her.

A tingle of disbelief raised goose bumps on her arms. She was getting married. That was what had happened to her.

Her office was in for quite a surprise.

Smiling, Madison picked up the phone, waited for the dial tone, punched in the number...

The line went dead.

Well, of course. You had to dial the international dialing code first, then the one for Manhattan. She did that...and, once again, found herself holding a dead phone in her hand.

Maybe she had the codes wrong. Or maybe you had to dial

for an outside line. Sahar would know or, if she didn't, she'd find someone who did. But where was Sahar? How was she supposed to summon her—and what an awful word that was! You summoned a taxi, not a person—

Someone rapped lightly at the door. Madison heaved a sigh of relief.

"Sahar. Please, come in. I was just thinking about—"

"My lady."

This wasn't Sahar. It was a man who looked even older than the sultan.

"My lady," he said in a quavery whisper, and bowed until Madison thought she heard his bones creak.

"Please, she said quickly, "stand up. You don't have to—"

"I am Fouad, Doorkeeper of the Golden Palace. What you might call the major-domo. His highness, the crown prince, thought you might wish to tour its rooms."

"Yes. Yes, thank you, I would but first… This telephone doesn't seem to work."

"Whom did you wish to call, my lady?"

Madison raised an eyebrow. None of your business, was her typically New York reaction, but Fouad was old enough to be her grandfather.

"My office," she said politely, "in—"

"Ah. That has been done."

"No, it hasn't. I haven't spoken to them since—"

"It has been done, my lady. My lord saw to it."

Madison raised her eyebrows. "The prince?"

"Yes. He took care of it."

"Well, that was good of him but I want to phone anyway, so if you'd just show me how to use this—"

"You are to see the palace, ma'am. The prince so commanded."

The prince had made a call she hadn't asked him to make. Had he also commanded she tour the palace, or was the old man's formal use of English putting the wrong spin on things?

"My lady?"

There was no sense in asking questions of Fouad. She'd save them for Tariq.

"I'd be happy to see the palace," Madison said pleasantly.

The old man made another of those backbreaking bows, followed by a sweeping gesture toward the door.

"If you would accompany me, please?"

Madison forced a polite smile and fell in beside him.

Walking through the palace was like walking through a dream.

High coffered ceilings. Frescoed walls. Blue-veined marble floors. Priceless paintings that surprised her by starting with Michelangelo and proceeding through Jasper Johns. Sculptures by Praxitales, Rodin and Brancusi. There were elegantly appointed sitting rooms, other rooms that held shiny banks of computers. The palace was filled with things as ancient as the desert, as modern as Manhattan, a dizzying blend that seemed to say time was as fluid as the waters that danced in the fountains of the exquisite gardens.

Or was that an illusion?

For all the signs of modern life, the Golden Palace was rooted in the past. Servants bowed as she passed; when she greeted them or asked their names, they responded politely but with heads bowed and eyes averted.

It was, Fouad said, as if he couldn't believe she didn't understand, the custom.

So was the way all conversation ceased when she entered a room. So was the way women curtsied. The custom, all of it…and a constant reminder of how different this world was from her own.

It was a sobering thought.

So was the realization that the palace, as beautiful as it was, was more a museum than a home. Did Tariq actually intend them to live here? The idea was not a happy one. What about New York? Did he have a place there, too? She assumed he did; she'd expected they'd live there…well, no. To be honest, she hadn't really thought about it.

Everything had happened far too quickly…maybe even including her acquiescence.

The tour lasted for what seemed hours. At the end, Fouad did another of those awful-looking bows.

"Please," Madison said quickly, "you don't have to do that!"

"It is the custom, my lady."

Was that the answer for everything in Dubaac? That it was the custom? What other customs were there? She wanted to ask Fouad or, after he'd shuffled backward out the door, Sahar.

But the maid said lunch was ready on the terrace and before Madison could say she wanted answers, not food, a girl who spoke no English curtsied and dipped and blushed her way into the room.

Madison signaled her to look up but it was pointless—the girl was obviously horrified by the suggestion.

"She is here to tend to you, my lady," Sahar explained. "To ready you for tonight. She will draw your bath, do your nails and your hair, as is—"

"The custom," Madison said, more sharply than she'd intended. "But *my* custom is to do things for myself."

"That is not our way."

"And all this—this bowing and scraping is? At least, I don't see you crawling on your hands and knees!"

Sahar's eyes narrowed. "No one crawls," she said carefully, "we simply do what is—"

"Don't say it!"

The woman looked at Madison as if she'd lost her mind. Madison swung away and tried to think. Was she crazy? Maybe. If not, why would she have agreed to become Tariq's wife without at least asking him where they'd live, what he expected of her...

The girl was whispering frantically to Sahar. Madison turned and looked at them, her temper growing even shorter at the pallor that had settled on the girl's face.

"Now what?"

"The girl wishes to know if she may do her job, my lady, or if she must report her failure to please you to Fouad."

Oh, for heaven's sake! Madison marched to a chair and sat down.

"Tell her to do whatever she'd been sent to do," she said, and for the next few hours, she endured the attention of the girl, of Sahar and, eventually, of half a dozen women while the distant sounds of arriving planes seemed to fill the sky overhead.

Finally, at dusk, Sahar looked her over, nodded in approval and sent the others away.

"It is time, my lady. I will dress you now."

"In what? I don't have—"

Sahar hurried into the dressing room and emerged a moment later with a garment wrapped in layers of tissue paper.

"Your gown," she said happily. "It arrived while you were with Fouad."

"It arrived?" Madison said stupidly. "How? From where?"

Sahar smiled as she gently removed the layers of paper, then eased the gown over Madison's head.

"Shoes, as well, my lady," she said, bending to slip a pair of high-heeled gold sandals on Madison's feet. "And all from Paris, of course, by plane, just like all the other things in your dressing room. Will you please turn, so I can do up these buttons?"

"Paris? Those things came from Paris? They weren't here all along?"

"Of course not," Sahar said with indignation. "The prince ordered them especially for you." Her voice dropped to a conspiratorial level. "It was a close call—is that how you say it? My lord had so little time, because of your elopement. The couturier did say this dress, your celebration dress, would be late... But it all worked out. After all, the prince *is* the prince. He can do magic!"

Stunned, Madison stared blindly at the mirror.

Magic, indeed.

Her husband had arranged for her kidnapping, for hundreds of thousands of dollars worth of designer clothing, for a gown for their wedding celebration, all in the certainty that she would do exactly as he wished.

What else had he arranged? The visit from his father and those touching sentiments? Tariq's sudden tenderness, his offer to set her free? Had it all been a lie, carefully choreographed to turn her into a docile wife instead of a woman determined to fight him?

Madison shuddered.

A little while ago, she'd asked herself if she were crazy. The answer was, yes, she had to be, to hand herself over to a man who had such power and used it so ruthlessly.

"Ohhh... Look at yourself, my lady. You are so beautiful! What a bride you will be tonight!"

Madison stared at her reflection. The gown *was* beautiful, a froth of cobalt-blue silk studded with tiny jewels, as if she were wearing a bit of the night sky. Small white orchids adorned her hair. Even her shoes were elegant, nothing but wisps of gold and jewels on high, slender heels.

Was this really she? Was this Madison Whitney, vice president of a Fortune 500 firm? Was this the woman with two university degrees? A woman the *New York Times* had referred to as someone who epitomized the success of women in business?

Madison spun toward her servant. Her obedient, it-is-the-custom servant.

"I want to see the prince!"

"You will, and very soon, my lady."

"I want to see him now!"

"That is not possible. The custom—"

Madison snatched the circlet of flowers from her head and flung it at the wall.

"Damn the custom! I will see Tariq now!"

"But a bride may not—"

"How is it you've suddenly started calling me a 'bride,' Sahar? Aren't I already married? Isn't that—that barbaric custom of stealing a woman and forcing her into a man's bed a wedding ceremony? Because if it isn't—"

"Oh! My lord!"

Sahar all but sank to the floor when the door swung open and banged against the wall as Tariq strode into the room. He wore a cream-colored uniform jacket over black trousers and boots; a single gold medallion blazed like the sun against the jacket.

"The doors here are thick, *habiba*," he said coldly, "but not thick enough to keep your angry words from spilling into the hall." He made a quick gesture; Sahar scurried away and he slammed the door after her. "What is happening here?"

"I've come to my senses," Madison said. "That's what's happening here! And I've finally realized what a—what a liar you are!"

He was on her in a heartbeat, catching her by the shoulders, drawing her to her toes, looking down into her face through eyes gone dark with rage.

"Do not," he said in a voice so soft and cold it was barely a whisper, "ever use such a word to describe me!"

"You had this all planned!"

"Of course I did. You knew that. How else was I to make you listen to me if I hadn't brought you on board my plane?"

"Kidnapped me, you mean!"

"I did it for a reason. I explained all of that to you and yet now, you call me—"

"You took it upon yourself to phone my office."

"Yes. I did." Tariq let go of her and folded his arms. "I thought the announcement of our 'elopement' might sound better, coming from me."

Madison stamped her foot in fury. "I do not need anyone to speak for me!"

"All right," he said, fighting to stay calm, "in the future, I won't."

"And then there's that dressing room. The clothes. This gown. Everything was here, waiting for me. You planned it all!"

So much for staying calm.

"Damn it, woman, I have not denied it! Would you have preferred I offered you rags to wear?"

He was right; she knew he was. Nothing had changed…and yet, everything had changed! Carrying her off in the heat of the moment was somehow not the same as all these signs of careful, cool-headed planning.

And it certainly wasn't the same as imagining that part of the reason he'd kidnapped her, even the smallest part, was that he'd suddenly realized how badly he wanted her.

"Well? Is that what you'd have preferred?"

Madison blanked her mind to everything but her anger at the situation this man, this—this arrogant man, had forced upon her.

"I would have preferred," she said, as coolly as he, "to have had a choice as to whether or not I wanted to marry you in the first place. Is that so damned difficult to understand?"

He glared at her, turned and strode away, then came back to where she stood.

"Perhaps something's gone wrong with your memory as well as your sense of reason. I *did* give you a choice, *habiba*. This morning. I offered to fly you back to New York, remember? To tell my father the truth, admit that you had not come with me willingly, that I really had taken you from New York against your will—"

"That you took me to your bed the same way!"

His eyes narrowed. "I took you to my bed because it was what you wanted."

"Liar!"

It was all the protest she had the chance to make. Tariq's mouth dropped to hers, covering it, capturing it, possessing it.

Madison struggled. Fought. Refused to give in to what she knew he wanted. She'd made enough mistakes; she would not make any more. Instead she forced herself to endure his kiss instead of tumbling into it as she ached to do, to stand unmoving even as her heart begged her to respond to him.

It worked.

Tariq lifted his head. Nothing showed in his eyes, not even anger. She had won, she thought, though the victory left her hollow.

"Tell your father the truth now," she said in a low voice. "That this was wrong. That it was never meant to be. That you are going to send me home because you regret what you did."

Tariq stepped back. "The only thing I regret," he said tonelessly, "is believing you cared for our child—and even, perhaps, for me."

"You're twisting everything, damn you! I'm not the one who started all this! I'm not the one who told such monstrous lies."

"I told you not to make such accusations about me."

Madison slapped her hands on her hips. "And I'm telling you, oh almighty sheikh, do not think you can control—"

She gasped as he pulled her into his arms again, as his hands rose to frame her face and imprison it.

"Fouad tells me you found our customs interesting, *habiba*. Well, here's another custom." His fingers tunneled into her hair; even in his blind fury he was aware that it felt like silk, that her skin smelled of flowers and sunlight. Another time, such things might have calmed him. Now, they only fueled his anger. "As my wife, you belong to me. You have no rights other than the ones I grant you. That is the way of things, in Dubaac."

"No." The word was a whisper. "Tariq. You wouldn't—"

"I would," he said harshly. "I already have. Five hundred guests have gathered to celebrate our union. If you think I am going to stand before them and tell them there is no union, that I have decided to let my American wife raise my child six thousand miles away from me, you are sadly mistaken."

Tears rose in Madison's eyes.

"You're lower than scum. A degenerate tyrant. And I hate you! I hate you, hate you, hate you—"

Tariq crushed her in his arms, kissed her mouth again and again, taking instead of giving, despising this woman for what she had made him become…

Despising himself, because she was right, this was all his fault. There were surely easier ways to secure his legal rights to his child.

But there was no easy way to secure his rights to the

woman who carried it and that realization thundered through him with each beat of his heart.

When he let her go, Madison wiped the back of her hand over her lips.

"You will never touch me again," she said in a trembling voice. "Never, as long as I live."

Tariq smiled. It was a smile of such awareness, such intimate knowledge, that it brought a rush of pink to her face—and despair to her heart.

After all this, she still wanted him. And he knew it.

"I will touch you, *habiba*," he said huskily. "We both know that."

"Sex," she said dismissively, "that's all it—"

Tariq bent his head and kissed her. *Don't respond*, Madison told herself, *oh, don't…*

And she wouldn't have, had his kiss been one of domination. But it wasn't. Despite their harsh words, his kiss was soft on her lips.

"Sex is passion," he murmured. "And passion is life." He met her eyes and lay his hand gently over her still-flat belly. "And then there is this child you carry. Our child. Would you really want me to be the kind of man who would walk away from it, and from you?"

He could see her struggling for an answer. Well, he was struggling, too.

Perhaps he was the things she'd called him.

But maybe—maybe he was only a man who knew, deep in his heart, he would have wanted this woman even if she weren't pregnant with his baby.

And maybe he was too much a coward to admit it.

CHAPTER TEN

IN THE end, there was no sense fighting him.

What Tariq wanted for her baby was what Madison wanted, too.

It was one thing to raise a child without a father when the father was unknown, but that had all changed. She couldn't deny her baby its parents.

Tariq sent Sahar to her. The woman did whatever small touch-ups had to be done, then smiled and fell into a deep curtsy.

"You look beautiful, my lady," she said softly. "May you and my lord the sheikh share a long and happy life."

Madison forced an answering smile. A happy life? Her child would have a mother and a father. She would have a husband whose sexual hunger for her had aroused a response that still shocked her…but was that happiness?

What about love? She'd never looked for it, never even imagined finding it because, as life had taught her, marriage wasn't about love…

Sahar opened the door and smiled at her. "My lady?"

Madison's heartbeat kicked into overdrive. No, she thought, no, she couldn't do it. Couldn't become the wife of a stranger…

"*Habiba*?"

Tariq was waiting for her, his eyes silver, that little muscle ticking in his jaw.

Why—why, he was nervous, too!

Of course he was. He had no more expected his life to take this turn than she had.

He held out his hand. She looked at it, then looked into his eyes and realized they were no longer the eyes of a stranger. They hadn't known each other long but she knew more about him than many brides knew about their grooms, thanks to the raw intensity of the past few days.

She knew, for example, that he was a man of honor. That he was responsible.

That he was beautiful Tall. Ruggedly handsome. Tender and strong and passionate…

"*Habiba*." His voice was rough. "I will do everything I can to make you happy. I swear it."

She knew that he meant it. Was that the reason for the tears that rose in her eyes? Slowly she put her hand in his. He brought it to his mouth, pressed a light kiss into her palm, folded her fingers over it.

Then he slipped his arm around her waist and led her through the palace, to the moment that would join them forever.

The grand ballroom was lit like the sunburst of a thousand stars.

Crystal chandeliers hung from the high ceiling, dazzling the eye. Candelabra on the elegantly set tables stood ready to cast a softer light during dinner.

A string quartet played Vivaldi in the background.

Guests stood chatting in small groups, some in the native costumes of Dubaac but most in the kinds of clothes New Yorkers would wear to a gala at the Waldorf.

Madison must have made a small sound of surprise because Tariq drew her closer.

"What did you expect, *habiba*?" he whispered. "Riders on horseback? Bonfires?" He grinned before she could answer. "It's all right, sweetheart. The truth is, that will all come later. Even the most sophisticated of my people still love some of the old ways."

Fouad, wearing a gold *dishdashah*, stood at rigid attention at the top of the marble steps that led to the ballroom floor.

"My lord, shall I announce you?"

"Yes—but what you shall *not* do," Tariq said quickly, before the old man could contort himself, "is that nonsensical bowing and scraping." He caught the look on Madison's face. "Ah, sweetheart, you give yourself away. You think I demand these things of my people."

She looked straight at him. "Don't you?"

God, he loved her honesty. Her courage and fire. He wanted to gather her to him, bend her back over his arm, kiss her until that look of apprehension left her eyes.

He had been wary, too. After all, this was a commitment he had not intended.

And then Madison had stepped out of the guest suite; he'd looked at her and thought, *This woman is mine*, and his nervousness had given way to something, a sense of joy, of happiness unlike any he'd ever imagined.

"No," he said quietly, "I don't. I know that not all traditions are good but *you* must know that it is not easy to change the habits of centuries."

Her eyes held his for what seemed forever. Then she touched the tip of her tongue to her lips.

"I—I will be a good wife to you, Tariq," she whispered. "I promise."

He knew it was wrong. In these circumstances, a man did not kiss his wife until after the formal announcement of their marriage had been made to those who were assembled for the event.

It was not the custom.

To hell with customs, he thought with sudden ferocity, and he gathered his bride in his arms, bent his head to hers and kissed her.

There was a second's shocked silence. Then the crowd began to applaud. Applause gave way to cheers and as it did, Madison cupped Tariq's face in her hands, brought his mouth to hers again and gave up denying what her heart had known all along.

She was in love, deeply in love, with her husband.

The night was a dream made of magic.

The sultan appeared. He welcomed the guests, spoke of Dubaac's bright future, of his love for his son and his delight that he had taken a wife.

He reached for Tariq's hand and Madison's, and joined them together.

"You bring joy to our people. We wish you all the happiness in our hearts."

Tariq turned Madison toward him. "My wife," he said softly.

"My husband," she whispered back, and he took her in his arms and kissed her again.

"An official kiss," he whispered against her mouth, and she laughed and wondered how she had ever feared letting this happen.

The hours flashed by.

Madison moved from guest to guest. She talked with an

actor she'd seen in a dozen films, chatted with the foreign minister, with an official from the UN. She spoke with a tall, ruggedly handsome man who said his name was Salim and that he was her husband's oldest and closest friend until another tall, ruggedly-handsome man cut in and said no, that wasn't true, his name was Khalil and *he* was her husband's oldest, closest friend.

They said those things solemnly, but their eyes were alive with laughter. Madison laughed, too, especially when Tariq came up beside her, put his arm around her and said that they were not his friends at all, they were notorious pains in the backside and the only reason he tolerated their presence was that he felt sorry for such pathetic cases.

Her father-in-law, the sultan, saved her by clasping her hand and drawing her away so he could introduce her to the American ambassador.

Khalil and Salim grinned at each other, grabbed Tariq by the elbows and hustled him into the next room.

"You sly dog," Khalil said, once the door was closed. "You told us you were looking for a wife but you never said a word about finding one."

"The Sahara Stud strikes again," Salim said, trying—and failing—to look serious.

Tariq thought about telling them the whole story but it was too long, too involved...too personal, even to share with these guys.

Instead he sighed, folded his arms, leaned back against the doorjamb and said they were just envious.

"Envious?" Khalil said.

"Envious."

"Well, she's beautiful, all right, but—"

"But?"

He looked at Salim. "Help me out here, damn it," he growled.

Salim grinned. "She's gorgeous, man—but we're in no rush to give up our freedom. A woman can be spectacular but that doesn't mean a man wants to tie himself down forever. Not that we're saying you shouldn't," he added quickly. "I mean, I mean—"

"He means," Khalil said helpfully, "we know you didn't have a choice. You were told you had to find a wife and so you... Oh, hell, I didn't—"

"It's okay," Tariq said, with a little smile. "I *did* have to find one but then fate stepped in and—"

"And?"

He hesitated. And fate had brought him a gift he'd never imagined finding. It had brought him a woman that he—a woman that he—

"Tariq?"

Tariq blinked. He looked at the two men who were his best friends, cleared his throat and threw his arms around their shoulders.

"It's been great, seeing you two, but I have to go."

"Go? Go where?"

"To find my wife," Tariq said, a little hoarsely.

Another quick bear-hug. Then, he hurried from the room leaving behind two men with puzzled expressions on their handsome faces.

"You think he's—I mean, you don't think he's in love with her?" Salim finally said.

Khalil snorted. "No," he said quickly.

Too quickly. The men looked at each other, shuddered at the possibility such a thing could happen to anyone they knew and loved, and went back to the party.

The night, after all, was young.

* * *

The night was young.

Too young.

Too much time to think.

Right now, for instance. Madison was standing with a small group of Americans, laughing at something one of them had said because everyone else was laughing, but her thoughts were elsewhere.

She'd seen Tariq's friends hurry him across the ballroom. She'd seen the door shut behind them.

What were they talking about?

Was Tariq explaining how he'd had no choice but to take her as his wife? Were his friends offering sympathy, assuring him he'd done the right thing even if he wished it hadn't been necessary?

"—beautiful country, your highness. Have you had the chance to see it yet?"

She forced her attention to the woman who'd addressed her. "Sorry?"

"I was saying, the river valley is just magnificent. Lush, very green, such a contrast to the desert that—"

The door opened. Tariq stepped into the ballroom. He stood still, looked around…

Madison's skin tingled. Was he looking for her? Yes. Their eyes met. Even at this distance, she could feel the heat of that gaze.

The woman kept talking as Tariq made his way across the crowded floor. People spoke to him; he nodded, said a few words but he never stopped until he reached Madison's side.

"Good evening."

His tone was even, his arm light as he slid it around her waist, but when she looked at him, she could see past the polite smile on his lips to the hot darkness in his eyes.

The American dipped her knees in a quick curtsy. "Your highness. I was just telling Miss Whit...your wife how beautiful the river valley west of the city is."

"Beautiful, indeed," Tariq said.

His hand splayed over Madison's hip. The gesture was simple, yet it spoke clearly of possession. Madison, who had never imagined wanting to be possessed by any man, felt her pulse quicken.

"You must show her how lovely it is, your highness!"

Tariq moved his hand slowly up Madison's spine, curled his fingers gently around her nape.

"There is much that I must show my wife."

Madison could hear the sudden roughness in his voice. His hand slid back down to her waist and he drew her closer.

A tremor went through her. Their eyes met again; what Tariq saw in his wife's face almost drove him to his knees.

She wanted him.

Wanted him, as much as he wanted her.

He knew what he had to do. Say a polite good-night to these people. Point out that it had been a long day. Clasp his wife's hand, lead her slowly from the room; no need to hurry because they were now officially husband and wife...

"Madison," he said softly.

She looked up at him. "Yes," she whispered, and it was all he needed her to say.

To hell with protocol and decorum and tradition. He was a man who wanted his wife; his wife wanted him, and it was time they did something about it.

"*Habiba*," he said, and he scooped her into his arms and kissed her.

A gasp rose from the little group gathered around them; it

grew into a shocked murmur as Madison wound her arms around her husband's neck and buried her hot face against his throat.

Someone gave a delighted giggle. Someone else laughed, and still someone else broke into applause that was instantly picked up by the crowd as his highness, Sheikh Tariq, the Crown Prince of Dubaac, carried his wife—his bride—from the ballroom.

He carried her through the palace corridors, up the wide staircase, down an endless hall and, at last, stopped outside the doors that led to his suite.

A uniformed palace guard snapped to attention. He reached for the ornate doorknobs but Tariq shook his head.

"Go," he said gruffly.

The guard saluted and hurried away.

Tariq shouldered a door open, stepped into his darkened sitting room, then kicked the door shut behind him.

His heart thundered. At last, he was alone with his wife.

Moonlight spilled across the silk carpet. He followed that delicate gossamer river into his bedroom and slowly lowered Madison to her feet.

"*Habiba*," he said thickly.

His hands framed her face, lifted it to his. He kissed her gently, softly, moving his lips against hers, loving the silken glide of her tongue, the scent of her skin.

There were flowers in her hair. He plucked them from the lustrous strands, let the blossoms drop at her feet.

"Tariq," she whispered, just that, his name, but the need in her voice was almost more than he could bear.

"Tell me," he whispered. "Tell me you want me."

She rose to him. Cupped his face. Brought his mouth to hers. Told him with her kisses that she wanted him.

Still, he needed to hear the words.

"Tell me," he insisted.

"I want you. Oh, God, I want you! Make love to me, Tariq. Please, don't make me wait…"

Tariq groaned. Captured her mouth. Kissed her again and again, his kisses growing more passionate as her lips clung to his.

He had been with a lot of women. He had known desire, known hunger, but never like this. His soul-deep need for her stunned him with its intensity. He wanted to kiss her forever, to drown in her taste, give his senses over to the sweetness of her mouth.

Most of all, he wanted these moments to last.

The first time had been too quick. The passion of it had left him shattered but he wanted more. He wanted—he wanted—

Madison moved against him. She was making the kind of little sounds that would surely drive a man wild.

Wait, he told himself fiercely, wait…

Instead, he slid his hand under her gown. Her legs were bare, her skin smooth and warm. She gasped as he moved his palm against her thigh and when she gave a hot little cry, his body clenched almost painfully.

He found the edge of her panties.

Silk. Silk and lace. Soft, but not as soft as she was. As the inner flesh of her thighs. As the bud he sought and found when he slid his fingers beneath the lace.

Madison jerked in his arms. "Tariq…"

"Yes," he whispered in a voice hardly his own, and he cupped her, felt the delicacy of the curls that guarded her feminine heart, felt the wetness of her desire burn against his palm.

He stroked her.

A wild cry burst from her throat; her head fell back; he saw her eyes, dazzling pools of deepest chocolate.

The room spun around him.

"Madison," he said, "*habiba…*"

"Please," she said brokenly, "please, Tariq, please, please, please…"

And, just that quickly, his control snapped.

He said something raw and savage. He pushed up her skirt, tore away the scrap of lace and silk that kept him from her, unzipped his trousers, lifted her in his arms and drove straight and deep into her slick, female heat. Her legs wrapped around his hips and she came instantly, her cry of surrender rising into the night sky like a shooting star.

Her teeth sank into his shoulder; he felt the quick, sharp bite and reveled in sharing the sweet pain of her fulfillment.

"Yes," he said, "yes, yes, yes…"

She brought her mouth down to his, kissed him, dug her fingers into his dark hair as the frenzy of another orgasm tore through her.

And, at last, Tariq let go, let his seed pump deep into his wife's womb.

Her head fell against his shoulder. She was slick with sweat, trembling in his arms.

"Tariq," she whispered.

"I know," he said, because he did.

He knew there had never been anything like what had just happened between them before, that the universe had stilled for the instant of their joining.

And, as he carried her to his bed—to their bed—he knew, too, that this was what he'd wanted all along.

Not just sex, but all it meant within the bonds of marriage. The promise that came of her heart racing against his, of his child growing in her womb.

Most of all, he knew that it was no longer important that

he was the Sheikh of Dubaac or the Crown Prince of an ancient kingdom.

What mattered was that he was a man and that this woman, this beautiful, difficult, generous, incredible woman, was his until the end of time.

CHAPTER ELEVEN

MADISON lay in her husband's arms.

He had drawn the covers up over them. To do that, he'd had to let go of her; she'd thought he was moving away so she'd reacted with instinctive pride and moved first…

But he hadn't let her.

"Hey," he'd said softly, "where are you going?"

And he'd reached for her, tucked her head on his shoulder and held her close against him.

"Okay?" he'd whispered.

"Yes," she'd answered, and what a pathetic answer it was. There had to be a better way to describe the way it felt to lie like this, her body pressed to the length of his, his heart beating under her palm, his scent, a glorious blend of man and sweat and sex, in her nostrils.

Tariq raised his head from the pillow, leaned in and kissed her mouth.

"You're sure it wasn't too quick?"

Madison blinked. He'd been talking about what they'd just done. About making love. Well, how could she have known? He'd used the word "okay," and "okay" didn't come close.

Making love with him had been wonderful.

"Sweetheart? Was it too quick?"

She smiled, touched her finger to his beautiful mouth and traced its outline.

"It was wonderful. *You* were wonderful."

"I'm not looking for compliments." He flashed a slow, sexy grin. "But I'm glad to get them."

She laughed. He did, too. Who would have thought laughter could be a part of what happened in bed? Her mother's life had made sex seem like a series of transactions. Her own limited experience had been—was there such a word as "underwhelming"?

Was this the difference between having sex with a man you liked and making love with one you adored?

"What?" he said, when he saw the color rise in her face.

"I was just thinking that—that making love with you was—it was—"

Tariq kissed her tenderly. "For me, too," he said gruffly. "It was like nothing I've ever known."

He gathered her closer, stroked his hand lightly down her body, luxuriating in the feel of her against him.

"There was no one in your life when we met?"

"No. There wasn't anyone for a very long time."

Tariq's heart soared. "That's good." Good? It was the understatement of the year. "That's perfect," he said, and kissed her.

The kiss began gently but as her mouth softened under his, he felt his hunger for her returning. He wanted her with an intensity that still surprised him.

What if he told her that? If he said, *Madison, I know I forced you into this marriage but you need to know that I—that I—*

That he what?

There was something in his heart, right within his grasp. A feeling. An emotion…

Taking a wife was his duty. He had been raised to understand that, and it had become even more important after Sharif's death. He understood that, too.

Marriage was required of him.

But not this.

Not this feeling of delight, each time he looked at his wife. Not this flood of happiness in his heart. Not the sense that he was standing on the very edge of a cliff and the wrong word, an unintended admission, could send him tumbling over the edge.

And certainly not the knowledge that if he did look into his heart, if he did say the words he'd never imagined saying, he would make himself the most vulnerable man in the world because how could he know what his wife really felt for him?

"Tariq? What are you thinking?"

Madison was looking at him. He met her eyes. He could feel it building within him again. The hunger. The desire. The need to possess her and make her his.

But not yet.

Not until he had taken the time to explore every sweet hollow, every part of her that awaited his touch.

"I am thinking," he said softly, "how very beautiful you are, *habiba*."

"What does that mean. *Habiba*?"

"It means sweetheart."

"That's nice." She smiled. "And you're beautiful, too."

He made a face. "Men aren't—"

"You are." She put her hand against his cheek, loving the slight roughness of his five-o'clock shadow. "Your face. Your body. So beautiful."

He caught her hand, kissed her fingers, folded the kisses into her palm.

"I can't take credit for any of it. I have my mother's features."

"Is she—"

"Yes." His smile tilted. "She died when Sharif and I were very young."

"I'm sorry, Tariq."

He shrugged. "I am, too, but she was not really a part of our lives. Our parents raised us according to…"

"Tradition," Madison said, and sighed. "Custom."

He nodded. "We had nannies, then governesses, and then we were sent away to private schools in the States." He dropped a light kiss on her mouth. "I don't want that for our child, *habiba*. I want us to raise him. Not people we pay to do it."

"Maybe."

His eyebrows rose. "Maybe?"

"Maybe it won't be a 'him,' Tariq. Maybe it'll be a 'her.' And if it is—is there a custom that applies to the status of girls as heirs to their father's throne?"

She was smiling, but he knew the question was a serious one and that it deserved a serious answer.

"There is." He leaned over her and kissed her mouth. "In which case, *habiba,* we'll break another tradition and raise our daughter exactly as we would have raised a son."

"Good. Very good. Because though I understand the need for traditions—"

He took her mouth in a slow, deep kiss. "Some traditions don't need to change," he murmured.

"Like this one," Madison said softly. He felt her lips curve against his. "I agree."

"There are others, sweetheart."

Tariq kissed her throat. Pressed his lips to the hollow of it, where her pulse had begun to race.

"Show me," she sighed.

He cupped her breast. Watched her eyes darken as he

rubbed his thumb over its beaded tip. Felt an almost savage rush of joy spread through him when she cried out as he lowered his mouth and drew the nipple into his mouth.

"Do you like this?" he said gruffly.

She answered with a little catch of the breath, then another as he kissed her navel, her belly. When he brushed his lips against the golden curls at the juncture of her thighs, she trembled.

"Open your legs for me," he said, his voice as thick as honey. "Like that. Yes. Let me see you, sweetheart. Let me… There. Right there. That perfect flower, blooming only for me."

She cried out as he put his mouth to her, licked her, sucked her, stroked her gently until she was sobbing his name, begging him to make love to her.

Tariq knelt between his wife's thighs.

"Look at me, Madison," he said.

Her eyes locked on his face. Slowly, so slowly he thought it might kill them both, he slid into her. Deep into her. Seated himself in her heat and began to move.

She wept, and he kissed the tears. She sobbed his name and he caught the sobs with his mouth. She moved beneath him, wrapped her legs around him, and when they came this time, when they fell into that place where hearts and bodies become one, Tariq knew he was surely the luckiest man in the world.

Sometime during the night, Madison woke from a deep sleep.

Sounds had awakened her. Deep vibrations that seemed to echo through her blood.

"Fireworks," Tariq murmured. "You can see them out the window."

She sat up and scooted to the edge of the big bed as the sky lit with color.

"Ohhh, Tariq! How beautiful!"

She was what was beautiful, he thought, and reached for her, but she had already grabbed a small blanket from the foot of the bed, wrapped it around herself and hurried to the window.

Tariq sighed, sat up and ran his hands through his hair. "All right," he said without much enthusiasm, "we'll watch for a while."

But by the time he'd joined his bride, her obvious delight in the lightshow arcing high over the palace made him smile. He put his arm around her.

"Is this display for you?"

"For us, *habiba*. Do you want to go out on the terrace?"

She looked down at herself, then at him, standing beside her unabashedly naked.

"Like this?"

Tariq grinned. "Exactly like this. The fireworks are down on the beach. No one will see us, I promise."

The night was warm; the air carried the scent of the sea. Tariq held back a little as Madison looked over the terrace wall.

Another burst of color, this time made of pink and purple chrysanthemums, filled the sky.

"Look," she said happily, "have you ever seen anything so wonderful as this?"

No, he thought, he hadn't. But he wasn't looking at the fireworks; he was looking at his wife. At her golden hair, spilling over her shoulders. At the elegant line of her naked back, visible above the low dip of the blanket.

He saw more.

Her incredible spirit. Her concern for others. Her selflessness in first wanting a child to raise alone, then in agreeing he had the right to be that child's true father, even if it meant turning her own life upside down.

Most of all—most of all, he saw what was in his heart.

He loved her.

He loved his wife.

Tariq's throat tightened. He went to her, put his arms around her and drew her back against him.

"*Habiba*," he said softly.

Something in his voice made the fireworks suddenly not as important as they had been. Madison turned in her husband's arms. Looked into his eyes. What she saw there made her heart soar.

"Tariq," she whispered.

Slowly, his eyes never leaving hers, he lowered his head and kissed her. She sighed, put her hands on his chest and kissed him back. The sweetness of the kiss brought tears to her eyes. She said his name again as she wound her arms around his neck, and he picked her up and carried her into the bedroom, to the bed.

The blanket fell from her like the petals of a flower. Tariq kissed her throat, her breasts, her belly. He kissed her everywhere, with passion and yet with a tenderness that brought every sense alive.

This time, when he entered her, he did it slowly. He watched his wife's lovely face, saw the pleasure he brought her reflected in her eyes.

He moved deep within her, moved until she cried out and he felt the faint convulsions of her womb.

"Tariq," she said, and he kissed her and kissed her, slid his tongue against hers and moved inside her silken heat again, took her over the edge again, glorying in the knowledge that he loved her, that he could do this to her, for her...

She reached between them, cupped his scrotum. He shuddered, groaned, fought for control...

"Please," she said, "please, come with me…"

And, at last, body glistening with sweat, Tariq followed his wife into the star-shot darkness.

Sahar woke them in late morning, tiptoeing around the room, setting a tray that held a coffee service on a bedside table.

Tariq yawned and sat up.

Madison gasped, rolled on her belly and burrowed under the covers.

He laughed as Sahar shut the door quietly behind her.

"Is this how you always greet the day, *habiba*? With your head under the blanket?"

"Is she gone?"

Tariq grabbed the covers and yanked them down. Madison gave an indignant shriek.

"Yes, she's gone." He bent his head and kissed her nape. "Time to rise and shine."

"Does she always do that? Come straight into your room even if you—even if you—"

"You mean," he said solemnly, kissing his way down her spine, "is this another of our customs? Well, someone always brings me morning coffee, yes." He reached her bottom, dropped a light kiss on each rounded cheek. "But there is no 'even if' involved here, sweetheart." Gently he rolled Madison onto her back. "I've never brought a woman to these rooms."

Why did that make her feel so good?

"No?"

"No." He touched the tip of his finger to the tip of her nose. "And stop looking so smug."

"I am not looking smug, I'm looking…"

"Pleased," he said softly.

She smiled. "Yes."

"And happy."

She smiled again. "Very."

Now, he thought, tell her now. Take her in your arms. Say, *Wife, I love you. I adore you...*

But, God, it was such a terrible risk.

A man said those words to a woman, he wanted her to say the same words to him. Not that he'd really expected that, in a marriage. Marriage, for a man like him, had to do with matters of state.

Who could have known his marriage would have to do with matters of the heart?

Who could have known he'd be such a coward?

At fifteen, he'd been flying single-engine aircraft for two years. At eighteen, he had his pilot's license. At twenty, he flew his first jet.

Name the extreme sport and he'd tried it. Rock-climbing. Skiing on glaciers. Sky-diving, running the most difficult rapids, crossing the Alahandra Desert on foot with Sharif, Khalil and Salim, half a dozen bottles of water and nothing else just because people said it couldn't be done.

He had filled his life with risk.

But this was the greatest risk of all and he could not take it yet because if his wife didn't love him—if she didn't—

If she didn't, would he love her enough to set her free? Wouldn't that be the right thing to do?

No. There was their child to consider. The child they agreed should have two parents...

"Tariq?"

No matter what, the child came first. Besides, Madison said she was happy...

"Tariq. What's wrong?"

He looked at his wife. She was sitting up against the pillows, a shadow of concern in her eyes.

"Nothing's wrong," he said. He reached for her, gathered her against him and pressed a kiss to her hair. "I was just thinking—I was thinking that I am happy, too."

Madison closed her eyes and burrowed against her husband. If only he'd said he loved her. Oh, if only!

But she would not be greedy. Fate had already brought her a man she adored, and his child in her womb.

For all she knew, there might well be a limit to how many miracles a woman could expect in one lifetime.

The morning raced by.

Coffee in bed. Brunch on the terrace. Madison wasn't very hungry.

"I ate enough for an army last night," she said, with a quick smile, though she really hadn't. Last night, she'd been too nervous, too excited to eat. Now, she was simply too happy.

In early afternoon, he asked if she wanted to see the city.

"Oh, yes," she said, "I'd love that!"

He dressed in faded jeans and a dark blue shirt with the sleeves rolled back on his forearms. She chose a pair of beige linen capris and a white silk T-shirt.

"Is this all right? If anyone should see us, will they think I'm breaking with some kind of custom?"

Tariq smiled and took her in his arms. "They will think I am a lucky man, *habiba*," he said softly. "And they will be right."

A red Ferrari waited at the foot of the palace steps. Tariq helped her in, then got behind the wheel.

"Your seat belt," he said.

Madison sighed dramatically. "Yessir."

He leaned over and kissed her. "You must tell me if you

grow tired, sweetheart." Gently he put his hand over her belly. "Yes?"

"Yes," she said, and wondered, fleetingly, if his concern was for her or for their baby—and wasn't that an awful way to think? He loved the baby; he cared for her. What did it matter if those two things weren't exactly the same?

Besides, she loved the baby, too. It was already real to her, even though the fetus was only a little more than a month old.

Dubaac turned out to be nothing she'd expected. It was a beautiful, modern city filled with soaring buildings, well-known hotels and glittering shops whose names she recognized from back home.

Tariq parked on a street filled with expensive shops. They strolled, hand in hand; people smiled at them, some dipped their heads in respect.

He drew her into a store filled with expensive gems.

The proprietor urged her to choose something.

"Anything the princess likes," he said. "Anything at all."

Tariq put his mouth to her ear. "It's all right, *habiba*," he whispered. "I'll pay for it. Go on. Choose something. That emerald, perhaps. Or this yellow diamond pendant. It's perfect with your hair and eyes."

But she didn't choose anything. Everything was too expensive, she whispered back.

He wanted to laugh, that his wife should think something like this was more than he could afford. In the end, to please the shop owner, he bought her the diamond and hung it around her throat.

She touched it with her hand and said it was beautiful.

And he thought, *Not half as beautiful as you.*

The street changed, took on the mystery of an earlier century. They had entered a *souk,* an ancient market crowded with shops and stands.

This time, it was Madison who drew Tariq to a counter. It was lined with small adornments made from things of the natural world. A seashell pendant. A bit of amber. A tiny, highly-polished stone and delicate feather that hung together from a finely plaited braid of something soft and shiny.

"How beautiful," Madison said softly.

Tariq smiled. She had made a choice he would have made himself. The stone came from the river that ran in the mountains that bordered the desert; the feather had fallen from the wing of a hawk; the braid was made of fine horsehair.

"It's a love fetish," he said. "An amulet. Something a man gives a woman he loves. Some of the tribal people still believe in such things. Do you like it, *habiba*?"

She nodded shyly. Tariq bought it, and put it into Madison's hand. Her smile lit her face—and his heart.

In the car again, they drove to a hill that looked out over the city.

Oil had brought Dubaac incredible wealth, Tariq explained, and in the last few years, his brother had convinced their father that the old ways could be made to blend with the new for the benefit of all the people.

Madison looked at her husband. "Did you agree with Sharif?"

Tariq nodded. "Very much. In fact, I wanted to make even greater changes. There are still some villages without plumbing or electricity, still elders who do not believe girls should be educated. Those things must change, and—" He flashed a sheepish grin. "Sorry. You asked a question. I answered with a speech."

"Not a speech," she said softly. "You answered with your heart and—and— Uh."

The little expulsion of breath was soft. Tariq cocked his head. "Madison?"

"It's nothing. Really. I just… I have a twinge in my back or something."

"Damn it, I should have realized… This car's not meant for a pregnant woman." He reached out and turned on the engine. "Let's go back."

"No, it isn't that. I…"

"*Habiba.* What is it?"

"A cramp. A sharp…oh. Oh God, Tariq! I think I'm bleeding…"

Tariq reached for her hand, caught it so tightly he all but crushed it in his as he sent the Ferrari leaping forward.

"You'll be all right, *habiba*," he said fiercely. "I swear it."

But, in the end, he was powerless to keep that pledge.

He was the Crown Prince. The sheikh of a wealthy and important nation. The financial world followed his investments; his people hung on his every word.

For all of that, he could not help his wife.

Tariq had phoned ahead as he drove Madison to the brand-new hospital his brother had built in the newest section of the city; they were met by his private physician, trained in Paris, the head of obstetrics, trained in New York, and a team of nurses.

They put Madison on a gurney; she grabbed for Tariq's hand and held it tightly as they rushed her into an examining room.

His doctor had to peel his fingers from hers before he would let go.

A nurse closed the door.

And Tariq, always strong, always powerful, always in control, struggled not to fall apart.

Madison. His wife, without him on the other side of that door. Alone. Frightened. In pain.

"Please," he whispered, "please, keep her safe."

He paced the floor and when that changed nothing, he sank onto a bench and buried his face in his hands. The minutes became an hour, became two hours and he tried not to watch the clock because the hands weren't moving fast enough…or maybe they were moving too fast, and heaven only knew what time would bring.

Finally the doctors appeared.

Tariq shot to his feet.

"I'm sorry, your highness," his physician said quietly.

The world tilted. "My wife…?"

"She's fine, sir. But the baby…"

"It was what we call an early pregnancy failure, Sheikh Tariq," the obstetrician said.

Tariq shut his eyes. "It's my fault," he said, his tone low and anguished. "We argued. I put her through hell. I made her fly all this distance. And I made love to her…"

"My lord, I assure you, none of that had any effect on the pregnancy. This is a situation in which the embryo simply never developed." The doctor ran a hand through his thinning hair. "I could explain it in more clinical detail…"

"No. Please, Doctor. I appreciate your offer but… Not now."

"The important thing is that what happened was no one's fault. There's no reason for it to occur again, either. You and your wife can look forward to a normal pregnancy in the near future." The obstetrician's voice softened. "Just give her time to get over the emotional shock of the loss. If she seems a bit distant, that's to be expected."

Tariq nodded. "Yes. Yes, of course."

His private physician cleared his throat. "She may not show interest in sex for a while, sir."

Tariq's head snapped up. "Do you think I don't know that?"

"I'm only pointing out that—"

"I know what you're pointing out," Tariq said wearily, the fight gone from his words. "I assure you, Doctor, sex is the last thing on my mind now. I just want to be certain my wife is going to be all right."

"We'll move her to a private room and keep her overnight but, yes, she's going to be fine. Why don't you check for yourself, your highness? I'm sure the princess will be happy to see you."

Tariq nodded again. Then he took the most difficult step of his life. He opened the door to Madison's room went inside.

Oh God! His heart turned over at what he saw.

His strong, brave wife lay in a narrow bed, her face to the wall, a tube snaking from her arm.

"*Habiba*," he said softly.

She didn't move. He went to her, leaned down and brushed damp strands of hair from her forehead.

"Sweetheart. I am so sorry…"

She nodded. "I know."

Her voice was small but it pierced his soul with an anguish so deep he had to fight for the words that would somehow comfort her.

"There was nothing anyone could do."

She nodded again. "They told me that."

Tariq pressed his lips to the tracery of a vein in her temple. He could feel the pulse of her blood under the delicate skin.

"They want you to stay the night, *habiba*. I will stay with you."

"No."

"But sweetheart—"

"I don't need you with me, Tariq."

Her words hurt. He told himself he understood, that this was her way of fighting the emotional pain of their loss.

"All right. If that's what you want…"

"It is."

He nodded. He seemed to be doing a lot of nodding; perhaps that was all he was capable of right now.

"Very well, then. I'll make sure they put you in a quiet room, and when I pick you up in the morning…"

Her eyes were closed. Had she fallen asleep? Or did she simply not want to be with him right now?

He stepped back, fighting a momentary rush of anger. The baby had been in her womb, yes, but it was his child, too. He might not have felt the physical pain of losing it but the emotional pain was just as real.

And what kind of SOB would drop that on his wife right now?

Of course it was more difficult for her than for him. He understood that. And after he took her home tomorrow, he would do everything in his power to show her that they had lost their baby but they had not lost everything.

They still had each other.

Except, they didn't.

Days slipped past.

The doctors gave Madison the thumbs-up. She was fine. She could return to normal life, to whatever activities she wished.

Her primary activity seemed to be avoiding Tariq.

He knew he was awkward around her but, damn it, what did a man say to a woman who had lost the child she'd wanted so desperately that she'd gone to extremes to conceive it?

These things happen.

We can try again.

The first was so pathetic he couldn't bring himself to say it.

The second sounded like an excuse to get her back in his arms—and it was plain as day that being back in his arms was the last place she wanted to be.

The very first night home, she slept so far across the bed, all but clinging to the edge of the mattress, that they might as well have been in different rooms.

He wanted to reach out and gather her against him but he was afraid she'd think he wanted sex and, God knew, he didn't.

Not sex.

What he wanted was her. Madison. His wife, warm and sweet in his arms, but the doctor's warning was burned into his brain and Madison's own behavior reinforced it.

Out of bed, they behaved like polite strangers.

Madison walked the palace grounds. She sat on the beach, arms wrapped around her knees, and stared at the waves frothing against the shore. If he suggested lunch in town, she thanked him and said she wasn't hungry. She had the same reaction when he asked if she'd like to drive out to the desert.

She didn't wear the diamond he'd bought her.

Added up, even a fool could figure out that she didn't want anything to do with him.

After a while, he stopped asking her to go with him. He told himself it was to save her from having to fend off his suggestions but the truth was, it was to keep him from hearing her say no, she didn't want to go with him; no, she didn't want to talk to him; no, she didn't want to sleep in his arms…

No, she didn't want to be married to him.

Because that's what it was all about. By the end of the month, he knew it was time to admit it.

So he kept busy. Kept away from her, as much as was humanly possible. There were council meetings to attend. A new program of educational innovations to pursue. There were teleconferences with New York, faxes to read and approve, e-mails, phone calls…

He had a life he'd all but forgotten. Now, he plunged back into it, but nothing he did could blur the truth.

He had forced Madison into marriage. She'd made the best of it, for the sake of their baby.

But there was no baby anymore.

There was no reason for the marriage.

She knew it. After a while, he did, too.

He loved her. God, yes, he loved her with all his heart and soul.

The only question was, did he love her enough to do the right thing and set her free?

CHAPTER TWELVE

IT WAS a beautiful morning, the kind artists loved to capture on canvas.

Madison stood on the white sand beach of the Golden Palace, staring at the sea.

Sunlight reflected off the aquamarine water; far in the distance, a ship moved slowly against the cloudless sky.

What a perfect moment to share with Tariq, she thought.

And then she remembered she must not think that way. Not the beauty of the scene, not anything in the world could change the reality of what had happened.

She had lost a baby.

That would break any woman's heart, but she had lost even more.

She had lost her husband.

Tears burned her eyes. Madison blinked them back. She wept, or was on the verge of weeping, all the time. And there was no logic to it. Crying wouldn't change a thing.

Tariq had demanded she marry him because she was pregnant with his child. Initially she'd despised him for forcing her into becoming his wife. Then she'd begun to see that he'd done it for all the right reasons. After all, the child she'd carried had been as much his as hers.

Now, there was no child.

No reason for the marriage neither of them had wanted.

All of it was logical—except for one thing. One small, impossible thing.

She'd fallen in love with her husband.

He didn't love her. She'd always known that, though there'd been moments after he'd brought her to Dubaac, when she'd almost let herself think that he might, at least, have been falling in love with her.

Madison gave a hollow laugh as she began walking slowly along the shore, through the ankle-deep water that lightly kissed the sand.

It wasn't the first time she'd been that foolish.

Once, somewhere between her mother's second marriage and her third, a man she'd been seeing had taken to bringing Madison little gifts. A plush bear. A book of fairy tales. A single rose, just for her, when he brought a dozen of them for her mother.

"I think he really likes me, Mama," she'd confided shyly.

Her mother had smiled the way grown-ups do when they know the secrets of the universe.

"It doesn't have anything to do with liking you, Maddie," she'd said. "He's just trying to score points. You know. Do whatever might make things go better for him."

A tiny shorebird raced along the damp sand after a receding wave. Madison watched it poke at the sand and then run back to safety before the next breaker could snatch it and carry it out to sea.

She'd hated her mother for saying that. She'd told herself it wasn't true—but, when the affair between the man and her mother ended, he'd disappeared from Madison's life.

Her mother was right; he hadn't cared for her at all.

If only she'd remembered that lesson.

Yes, Tariq had laughed with her. Held her. He'd made love to her—it was such an awful cliché but she'd glimpsed paradise in his arms.

But "love" had nothing to do with it.

He'd done it all simply to make things go better. For himself and, she supposed, for her, too, because he was a decent man. He'd even tried to go on pretending their marriage still made sense, but it hadn't worked.

She'd seen through it, right away.

That day she'd lost the baby, it had seemed an awfully long time until he'd come into the examining room to see her.

Her heart had been aching over the loss of their child.

I'm sorry, he'd said, and he'd touched her cheek, put his lips to her brow but oh, what she'd have given for the whisper of his mouth against hers.

It would have meant the world, just one sweet kiss. It would have told her she mattered to him, even without his child inside her.

Not that he hadn't been kind.

He'd spoken gently. Offered to spend the night at the hospital with her. Offered, instead of just doing it but then, Tariq always managed to make the right move.

When she said "no," because she hadn't wanted him to feel he had to stay, he'd said all right, he'd see her in the morning.

But if he'd really cared for her, if she'd been more to him than a woman who'd carried his child, he wouldn't have asked. Or he'd have ignored that "no."

He'd have stayed with her, lain in the bed with her, held her in his arms and most of all, most of all he'd have whispered, *Habiba, I love you. I mourn for our child but you need to know that I love you, that I am happy I married you and I want you in my life now and forever.*

None of that had happened.

He'd come for her the next morning in his chauffeured limousine. Taken her back to the palace. That night, she'd crept into bed, desperate to turn to him and go into his arms but she'd felt like an impostor, a woman in a prince's bed who'd turned up there only because of an impossible set of circumstances.

And Tariq had not touched her. Not that night or the next and the next, not once since she'd lost their baby.

The man who had once made love to her with such fiery passion kept his distance as politely as a stranger. The man who'd once spent every minute by her side was too busy with meetings and phone calls to see her, except at dinner. Lately he'd given up on that, too, and sent Sahar to offer his regrets. He just couldn't spare the time…

"Madison."

She swung around, putting her hand to her face to sweep her wind-tossed hair from her eyes.

Tariq was walking toward her across the sand, tall and imposing and beautiful enough to make her heartbeat stumble.

There was a time she'd have run to him. Not now. Instead she wrapped her arms around herself as he approached her. His face was unreadable, his eyes hooded. Her stomach knotted and, in one of those moments no one can ever explain, she knew what he had come to tell her.

Why wait for him to make the first move?

She had nothing left except her pride.

"Madison. I've been looking for you."

"Have you?" She licked her lips. "I wanted somewhere quiet, where I could think."

The breeze had picked up in intensity. He shrugged off his

jacket and started to drape it around her shoulders but she stepped back. The last thing she wanted was a substitute for his arms, but only a fool would say that.

"Thank you," she said politely, "but I'm fine."

"Are you?" he said softly.

"Yes. Well, of course, things aren't the same as they were but that's to be expected." She hesitated. "Let's be honest, Tariq. When we lost our baby, we lost something else."

He nodded. She was being honest. It hurt, but her honesty was one of the things he'd fallen in love with.

"We lost the reason for our marriage," she said, and he knew everything had come to an end.

And that was why he'd come to talk to her, wasn't it? To tell her he was setting her free? But she was moving too fast. He wasn't ready. Not yet. Not yet…

"You forced me into marriage because I carried your baby. And now I don't."

Forced? Did she still think? Maybe he'd forced things, at first, but he'd never forced her to moan in his arms. And just before their marriage had been made legal, according to the traditions of his people, he'd given her a choice.

Stay or go, he'd said—and she had chosen to stay. To stay, with him…

"We both know the truth, Tariq. There's no reason for us to stay married anymore."

He looked at her. Her eyes glittered. He wanted to think it was with tears but perhaps it was with defiance. Not that it mattered. He'd come here to do exactly what she was doing.

He stopped thinking. Instead he closed the distance between them, clasped her shoulders, lifted her to her toes.

"Is that it?" he said roughly. "Is that all you have to say?"

"No. There's more." She swallowed. "I want to go home.

I want to go back to my life. I want out of this—this point-less marriage."

He growled, hauled her against him, kissed her hard and deep. She didn't respond. Not at first. Then she gave a little cry and opened her mouth to his, leaned into him, let his heat, his taste, his scent surround her this one last time before she put her hands against his chest, tore her mouth free of his and stepped back.

"Sex," she said, her voice trembling, "that's what we have without the baby. Nothing but sex—and it isn't enough."

His eyes swept over her face. There it was, at last. The truth of what she felt for him. Or what she didn't feel for him. Either way, it didn't matter. This had only been an interlude for her.

For him, too.

He didn't love her. He never had. When she'd carried his baby, he'd wanted to believe himself in love with her but the truth was, she was simply a woman who had passed through his life.

"You're right," he said briskly. "It isn't enough."

"Then—then you'll agree to a divorce?"

"I'll make the arrangements immediately." He cleared his throat. Anger, surely not any other emotion, had made his voice rough. "In fact, my plane will take you to the States this afternoon. I'll call my lawyer. He'll be in touch by the start of the week."

"Make sure he understands I want this done as quickly as possible."

"Arrangements for alimony might take some time."

Madison flung out her arms. "For what? For a marriage that never should have happened? I don't want alimony, damn it! I just want this over with."

Tariq wanted to drag her into his arms again. Kiss her. Force her to admit that there had been more between them than sex and a baby…

Except, there hadn't been. Their marriage had been all about passion and expedience, nothing more.

"In that case… We had a traditional wedding," he said coldly. "We need only a traditional divorce."

"Meaning?"

"Meaning…" He drew himself up. "Meaning, I, Tariq, Crown Prince of Dubaac, heir to the Golden Throne, sheikh of all my people, do hereby free you from all marital commitments and duties."

Madison blinked. "That's it?"

"Tradition," he said. "That's it."

She laughed. Then, before her laughter could turn to tears, she fled.

He was true to his word.

Two hours later, his plane took off with Madison on board, bound for New York.

She refused to take anything he had bought her. Tariq wanted to think it was because she was so damned independent but he wondered if it was because she didn't want to have anything to remind her of the days she'd spent as his wife.

Not that he gave a damn.

In the end, he'd seen the truth. That he had not loved her; he'd loved the *idea* of loving her because she'd been carrying his child.

He sent word to his father but no explanation, and informed Sahar that he would dine alone, in his sitting room.

Sahar was silent as she served his meal.

"Thank you," he said.

She didn't answer. Her mouth was set in a thin line. If he hadn't known better, he'd have thought she was expressing displeasure but she would not do such a thing.

Sahar believed in the old ways. In tradition. She was a servant, and a servant knew her proper place.

He had no appetite and he pushed his plate aside, virtually untouched. Sahar snatched it out from under his nose and all but slammed a dish of *baklava* on the table before him. A tiny bit of the pastry broke off and flew into his lap.

Tariq looked at her. He looked at the *baklava*. Then he looked at Sahar again.

"My apologies," she said.

Only an idiot would have believed that.

"Is there something on your mind?" he asked calmly

"No. Yes! Of course there's something on my mind," she snapped, "but I doubt if you want to hear it."

His eyebrows rose. This woman had been in the service of the royal family his entire life and this was the first time she'd been anything but polite and—hell—servile.

"You sent her away!"

"I sent…" His face darkened and he pushed back his chair and shot to his feet. "Do not push your luck! If you think I'm going to discuss my personal life with you—"

Sahar dug into her pocket, plucked something from it and dumped it on the table.

It was the yellow diamond pendant.

"She left this behind."

"She left everything behind. So what?"

"She did not leave everything!"

"Woman, so help me, if you say another word… What do you mean, she didn't leave everything?"

"The amulet. The love fetish. The feather, stone and horsehair pendant that cost, what, a hundred thousandth of what the diamond cost? She took it with her."

"I do not see that this is any of your—"

"No. That is correct, *my lord*," she said, giving his title a note of sarcasm that shocked him. "You do not see at all!"

Tariq narrowed his eyes. "I'm warning you, Sahar…"

"She left the diamond. She took the amulet." Sahar folded her arms and glared. "She wore the amulet. I know, because I had to fasten it for her. She was weeping. Her hands were trembling. She was too upset to do it herself."

Tariq felt the faintest stirring in his heart. "So?"

"So, Lord Tariq," Sahar said, as slowly as if he were a slightly backward child, "your wife—"

"She is no longer my wife. I said the words that dissolved the marriage."

"Your *wife*," Sahar said, as if the very idea that words could end a marriage were a joke, "left here in tears, wearing an amulet from the *souk* instead of a jewel worth a king's ransom." One bushy eyebrow rose. "Even a fool should understand what that means."

Tariq's mouth went dry. Was he a fool? Why would a woman choose a cheap trinket over something worth tens of thousands of dollars?

"Maybe," he said, "maybe she wanted a souvenir. Something to remind her how—how primitive this part of the world is."

"My lord." Sahar took a deep breath. "If you were not the sheikh, if you were not the Crown Prince, if you did not still hold the power of life and death in your hands…if none of those things were true, I would tell you that you are a fool not to realize that your wife loves you."

"She does not," Tariq said, ignoring everything else

because those were the only words that mattered. "And I do not love her."

"She loves you, my lord! And you love her. And if you don't go after her, you'll regret it for the rest of your life!"

Silence. Then Sahar seemed to realize all that she'd said. Her face paled; she dropped into a curtsy so deep Tariq had to clasp her hands to haul her to her feet.

"Forgive me," she stammered. "I don't know what came over—"

Tariq framed her plump face with his hands and pressed a smacking kiss on her mouth.

Then he ran from the room.

Madison had finally fallen asleep.

The drone of the engines had taken her to a place where she couldn't weep anymore, couldn't agonize over all she'd found and lost in such a very short time.

It was the change in the sound of the engines that woke her. They'd stopped; the plane was motionless. She sat up in her seat, pulled aside the curtains and peered out the window.

The plane was on an airstrip, engulfed in moonlight and silence.

Quickly she pressed the buzzer for Yusuf. Pressed it again but there was no response. She undid her seat belt, got to her feet and walked to the front of the cabin.

The cockpit door stood open. The pilot and copilot were gone. She was completely alone.

The hair rose on the back of her neck.

"Hello? Is anyone here?"

"I am here, *habiba*," a deep, familiar voice said.

Madison swung around. Tariq stood in the doorway, still as a big cat.

"What—what are you doing here?"

A quick smile touched his mouth. "Why, I have come to see you, *habiba*. I should think that was obvious."

"I don't…" She swallowed. "I don't understand. Where are we?"

"Paris. It's the most romantic city in the world, or so I've been told." He flashed another of those little smiles she'd always thought were so sexy. "But then, I've been here only on business." He paused. "I've never been here with my wife."

"I am not—"

He closed the distance between them until he was less than a touch away. She could see the end-of-day stubble on his jaw. She thought of how that stubble felt, when he made love to her.

I'll shave, he'd said, the first time she'd mentioned it, but she'd drawn him down to her and whispered that she didn't want him to shave, that she loved the feel of that sweet roughness against her breasts, her belly, her thighs…

Heat flooded her cheeks.

"What do you want, Tariq?"

Slowly he reached for her. Gathered her in his arms. "You," he said softly. "You're what I've always wanted, *habiba*."

"No. You don't. And I don't want—"

He kissed her. Kissed her and kissed her, until she had to kiss him back or die.

Her lips parted. Her breath sighed into his mouth. He groaned, drew her even closer against his hard body and, slowly, she slid her hands up his chest, over his broad shoulders and linked them behind his neck.

"Tariq," she whispered against his mouth as tears rose in her eyes. "Don't do this. Please. I beg you, don't—"

"Don't what, sweetheart? Kiss my wife? Hold her in my

arms?" His voice softened. "Those are a husband's privileges, *habiba*. Would you deny them to me?"

"You're not my husband. You divorced me, remember?"

Tariq smiled. "Did I? Who knows the legality of any of these old customs?"

"And our marriage? You said it was valid."

"It was…but just to make sure, we'll be married again. In New York, here in Paris…wherever you like." His arms tightened around her. "I love you, Madison. And you love me."

"I—I lost our baby. You don't need me as your wife any—"

He silenced her with another kiss, then cupped her face with his hands.

"I will always need you," he said fiercely. "I can't imagine life without you." His hands slid into her hair; he tilted her face to his. "I should have told you sooner. I should have said, 'Darling, I love you…' but I was afraid you weren't ready to hear it."

"But when I lost the baby…"

"I was heartsick. For the loss—and for you, *habiba*. I wanted to comfort you, to grieve with you, but…" He shook his head. "But I thought you didn't want me anymore, that in losing our child, you had lost the reason for our marriage."

"Oh, no! No, Tariq! I wanted your love more than ever but—but you were so distant… I thought, he doesn't need me, there's no reason for him to want to stay married to me any—"

He kissed her. Kissed her again and again.

"I love you," he said. "I adore you. Do you understand, Madison? I love you, with all my heart."

Madison tugged his head down to hers and kissed him. His beautiful, courageous, defiant bride kissed him. Tariq whooped, swept her up into his arms and laughed. Then he carried her to the door of the plane.

"She loves me," he said to the crew gathered at the foot of the steps. "My wife loves me."

The pilot, the copilot, the cabin attendant beamed.

And so, Madison was certain, did all of Paris.

EPILOGUE

Two years and ten months later:

"Tariq," Madison said, "you can't! Sharif is too young."

"A boy is never too young to learn to ride," her husband said, and grinned. "Just look at him, *habiba*. He's a born horseman."

Madison rolled her eyes. They were on the terrace of their New York apartment and her husband was holding their son on the back of a horse—a rocking horse that they'd given him on this, his second birthday.

"You're right," she said, laughing. "He is."

The baby was the image of his father, though his eyes were the same chocolate-brown as his mother's. He was what all babies should be: beautiful, healthy, bright…and completely, unequivocally loved.

Madison watched her husband and son for a few minutes. Then she took a camera from a table still laden with what remained of Sharif's birthday celebration: a cake with blue icing and yellow candles, cards from Dubaac and a big red truck that had been a gift from his grandfather.

"Smile," she said, and her husband and son grinned.

She looked at them, looked at the image she'd captured,

and her heart filled with joy. There were times she couldn't believe there was this much happiness in the world.

"Habiba." Tariq smiled at her. "What are you thinking?"

Madison went to him. She lifted their son from the rocking horse and kissed him. Then she put her mouth against her husband's and gave him a slow, deep, sweet kiss.

"That I love you," she whispered, "that I adore you, that I'm the happiest woman in the world."

"Hold on to that thought," Tariq whispered back.

The baby yawned and tucked his thumb in his mouth. As if on cue, Sahar stepped onto the terrace and took the baby from his mother.

"Time for the young prince's nap," she sang, and carried Sharif away.

Tariq chuckled as he drew Madison to him.

"She has excellent timing."

Madison tilted her head back and gave her husband a slow, sexy smile.

"So do you," she said softly.

Tariq's gray eyes turned silver as he swung his wife into his arms and carried her through the apartment, to their bedroom.

"I love you, *habiba*," he said as he shut the door behind them. "I always will."

And he showed her, with his heart, his body and his soul, that he meant every word.

MILLS & BOON®
Pure reading pleasure

JUNE 2008 HARDBACK TITLES

ROMANCE

Hired: The Sheikh's Secretary Mistress	978 0 263 20302 8
Lucy Monroe	
The Billionaire's Blackmailed Bride	978 0 263 20303 5
Jacqueline Baird	
The Sicilian's Innocent Mistress	978 0 263 20304 2
Carole Mortimer	
The Sheikh's Defiant Bride *Sandra Marton*	978 0 263 20305 9
Italian Boss, Ruthless Revenge *Carol Marinelli*	978 0 263 20306 6
The Mediterranean Prince's Captive Virgin	
Robyn Donald	978 0 263 20307 3
Mistress: Hired for the Billionaire's Pleasure	978 0 263 20308 0
India Grey	
The Italian's Unwilling Wife *Kathryn Ross*	978 0 263 20309 7
Wanted: Royal Wife and Mother *Marion Lennox*	978 0 263 20310 3
The Boss's Unconventional Assistant	978 0 263 20311 0
Jennie Adams	
Inherited: Instant Family *Judy Christenberry*	978 0 263 20312 7
The Prince's Secret Bride *Raye Morgan*	978 0 263 20313 4
Milllionaire Dad, Nanny Needed! *Susan Meier*	978 0 263 20314 1
Falling for Mr Dark & Dangerous *Donna Alward*	978 0 263 20315 8
The Spanish Doctor's Love-Child *Kate Hardy*	978 0 263 20316 5
Her Very Special Boss *Anne Fraser*	978 0 263 20317 2

HISTORICAL

Miss Winthorpe's Elopement *Christine Merrill*	978 0 263 20201 4
The Rake's Unconventional Mistress	978 0 263 20202 1
Juliet Landon	
Rags-to-Riches Bride *Mary Nichols*	978 0 263 20203 8

MEDICAL™

Their Miracle Baby *Caroline Anderson*	978 0 263 19898 0
The Children's Doctor and the Single Mum	978 0 263 19899 7
Lilian Darcy	
Pregnant Nurse, New-Found Family	978 0 263 19900 0
Lynne Marshall	
The GP's Marriage Wish *Judy Campbell*	978 0 263 19901 7

0508 Gen Std LP

Pure reading pleasure

JUNE 2008 LARGE PRINT TITLES

ROMANCE

The Greek Tycoon's Defiant Bride   978 0 263 20050 8
Lynne Graham

The Italian's Rags-to-Riches Wife *Julia James*   978 0 263 20051 5

Taken by Her Greek Boss *Cathy Williams*   978 0 263 20052 2

Bedded for the Italian's Pleasure *Anne Mather*   978 0 263 20053 9

Cattle Rancher, Secret Son *Margaret Way*   978 0 263 20054 6

Rescued by the Sheikh *Barbara McMahon*   978 0 263 20055 3

Her One and Only Valentine *Trish Wylie*   978 0 263 20056 0

English Lord, Ordinary Lady *Fiona Harper*   978 0 263 20057 7

HISTORICAL

A Compromised Lady *Elizabeth Rolls*   978 0 263 20157 4

Runaway Miss *Mary Nichols*   978 0 263 20158 1

My Lady Innocent *Annie Burrows*   978 0 263 20159 8

MEDICAL™

Christmas Eve Baby *Caroline Anderson*   978 0 263 19956 7

Long-Lost Son: Brand New Family *Lilian Darcy*   978 0 263 19957 4

Their Little Christmas Miracle *Jennifer Taylor*   978 0 263 19958 1

Twins for a Christmas Bride *Josie Metcalfe*   978 0 263 19959 8

The Doctor's Very Special Christmas   978 0 263 19960 4
Kate Hardy

A Pregnant Nurse's Christmas Wish   978 0 263 19961 1
Meredith Webber

0608 Gen Std HB

MILLS & BOON®
Pure reading pleasure

JULY 2008 HARDBACK TITLES

ROMANCE

The De Santis Marriage *Michelle Reid*	978 0 263 20318 9
Greek Tycoon, Waitress Wife *Julia James*	978 0 263 20319 6
The Italian Boss's Mistress of Revenge *Trish Morey*	978 0 263 20320 2
One Night with His Virgin Mistress *Sara Craven*	978 0 263 20321 9
Bedded by the Greek Billionaire *Kate Walker*	978 0 263 20322 6
Secretary Mistress, Convenient Wife *Maggie Cox*	978 0 263 20323 3
The Billionaire's Blackmail Bargain *Margaret Mayo*	978 0 263 20324 0
The Italian's Bought Bride *Kate Hewitt*	978 0 263 20325 7
Wedding at Wangaree Valley *Margaret Way*	978 0 263 20326 4
Crazy about her Spanish Boss *Rebecca Winters*	978 0 263 20327 1
The Millionaire's Proposal *Trish Wylie*	978 0 263 20328 8
Abby and the Playboy Prince *Raye Morgan*	978 0 263 20329 5
The Bridegroom's Secret *Melissa James*	978 0 263 20330 1
Texas Ranger Takes a Bride *Patricia Thayer*	978 0 263 20331 8
A Doctor, A Nurse: A Little Miracle *Carol Marinelli*	978 0 263 20332 5
The Playboy Doctor's Marriage Proposal *Fiona Lowe*	978 0 263 20333 2

HISTORICAL

The Shocking Lord Standon *Louise Allen*	978 0 263 20204 5
His Cavalry Lady *Joanna Maitland*	978 0 263 20205 2
An Honourable Rogue *Carol Townend*	978 0 263 20206 9

MEDICAL™

Sheikh Surgeon Claims His Bride *Josie Metcalfe*	978 0 263 19902 4
A Proposal Worth Waiting For *Lilian Darcy*	978 0 263 19903 1
Top-Notch Surgeon, Pregnant Nurse *Amy Andrews*	978 0 263 19904 8
A Mother for His Son *Gill Sanderson*	978 0 263 19905 5

0608 Gen Std LP

MILLS & BOON®
Pure reading pleasure

JULY 2008 LARGE PRINT TITLES

ROMANCE

The Martinez Marriage Revenge *Helen Bianchin*	978 0 263 20058 4
The Sheikh's Convenient Virgin *Trish Morey*	978 0 263 20059 1
King of the Desert, Captive Bride *Jane Porter*	978 0 263 20060 7
Spanish Billionaire, Innocent Wife *Kate Walker*	978 0 263 20061 4
A Royal Marriage of Convenience *Marion Lennox*	978 0 263 20062 1
The Italian Tycoon and the Nanny *Rebecca Winters*	978 0 263 20063 8
Promoted: to Wife and Mother *Jessica Hart*	978 0 263 20064 5
Falling for the Rebel Heir *Ally Blake*	978 0 263 20065 2

HISTORICAL

The Dangerous Mr Ryder *Louise Allen*	978 0 263 20160 4
An Improper Aristocrat *Deb Marlowe*	978 0 263 20161 1
The Novice Bride *Carol Townend*	978 0 263 20162 8

MEDICAL™

The Italian's New-Year Marriage Wish *Sarah Morgan*	978 0 263 19962 8
The Doctor's Longed-For Family *Joanna Neil*	978 0 263 19963 5
Their Special-Care Baby *Fiona McArthur*	978 0 263 19964 2
Their Miracle Child *Gill Sanderson*	978 0 263 19965 9
Single Dad, Nurse Bride *Lynne Marshall*	978 0 263 19966 6
A Family for the Children's Doctor *Dianne Drake*	978 0 263 19967 3